YOU CAN

CALL ME

CLOVER

YOU CAN CALL ME CLOVER

A DOG RESCUE STORY

DARCY KATE

Four Leaf Press LLC

Four Leaf Press LLC

For inquiries or more information, contact:
Four Leaf Press LLC
#1062 76 Fort Eddy Rd., Suite 1
Concord, NH 03301

First print edition 2024

Cover design by Andy Bridge
Interior design by Ashley Santoro

Library of Congress Control Number: 2023919923

ISBN 979-8-9882940-0-9 (paperback)
ISBN 979-8-9882940-1-6 (ebook)

www.darcykatewriter.com

YOU CAN

CALL ME

CLOVER

CLOVER

A sweet scent greeted my nose on my third morning alone. Where was that coming from? It smelled like breakfast. I had to find it.

Before I could get up to investigate, I was distracted by a cat lapping water from a puddle. I stayed still, lying on the cool, hard ground. I'd seen these sly animals before, and I'd learned to keep my distance. While seemingly cute and inviting, one swipe of a paw or hiss from their tiny mouth was enough to send me running. This one was fluffy, orange, and white, almost like me, but I wasn't about to be fooled by any similarities we might share. Even though I was roughly four times their size, I'd grown scared of cats. They often acted like they were the largest animal in the room, or in this case, the alley.

The cat scurried away as I stood and did my morning shake. A silent shake. There used to be a jingle when I did this, but I'd lost the noisemaker that used to be around my neck shortly after I'd left home. I didn't know where I was or where I was going, but it felt freeing to not be wearing anything. It felt freeing to be on my own.

But where did that sweet scent go? It reminded me of the smells that would drift from my last home's windows on slow fall mornings while I'd lie on the porch. Was it the same sticky sauce my old family used to spill onto their breakfast plates? My hunger pushed me forward to find out.

"Hey, you! Shoo!" someone yelled to me through a partially opened door.

I was off.

Catch ya later, tasty morning smells. I hope someone enjoyed you.

I settled by a large grassy area after stopping at an over-flowing trash container and snagging a paper bag filled with heavy scents I knew would make my tummy ache, but I downed the food without a second thought.

Following my questionable breakfast, I watched as people ran by on a path, many with water dripping off of their faces. Some went speeding by in one direction, while even more went in the other. I decided both directions must not be desirable if people were leaving so quickly, so I ran across the grass behind me and into the woods, ready to enjoy another day on my own.

LOGAN

Logan exited the back door of River Ridge Chicken after completing his eight-hour shift on Saturday.

"Any plans tonight?" his coworker, Seth, asked.

He wished he could respond with an enthusiastic "yes." Fall had arrived in his small New Hampshire town, and the evening would be more enjoyable if he wouldn't be alone.

"Nah, man. Just headed home."

"Okay, well, see you tomor—"

"Oh wow," Logan interrupted, "look at that."

Logan pointed over to a medium-sized orange dog with white markings devouring scraps from the trash outside of the Irish pub across the street.

"Oh, the dog? Yeah, I saw it earlier when I was out on my break. It doesn't seem very interested in people, I have to say, but it looks too cute to be a stray. Anyway, I've got to go. See you tomorrow," said Seth before getting into his car and driving off.

The coworkers' conversation didn't seem to disturb the dog who continued chowing down on her findings.

Logan slowly crossed the road while keeping an eye on the dog. He had to cross the street to get to his car anyway, so he figured he might as well see if he could get closer to the dog at the same time. While Logan had never had a pet during his sixteen years of life, he'd always had a soft spot for animals, especially dogs. His mother used to wear a necklace with a paw print and clover charm every day before she passed away when Logan was only seven.

"Hey, buddy…" Logan said in a low voice with an outstretched hand. The dog startled and stared but didn't retreat as Logan continued his approach. "I'm not going to hurt you. You're a hungry fella, huh?"

The dog wagged her tail low and took a step back.

"You must be thirsty after eating all of those scraps, huh, bud? Let me get you some water."

The dog's ears perked up upon hearing the word "water."

Logan opened the passenger door of his car and grabbed a bottle of water. To his surprise, the dog was right behind him when he turned back around, wagging her tail expectantly. "Okay, so you *are* thirsty. Let's try this…" Logan cupped his left hand and used it as a makeshift bowl for the thirsty pup.

The dog drank all of the water from Logan's hand. Then drank it all again. After three more refills, she sat and stared up at Logan.

"All right, so what should we do now?" Logan said aloud as he scratched behind the dog's ears and looked around to see if anyone happened to be around who might have an answer.

He decided to take out his phone and call Drew, his friend from school. Drew always had an answer for everything. It just seemed to come naturally to him. Just as he'd anticipated, Drew came up with a plan for Logan and the stray dog. Logan would take her to the nearby canine rescue.

"Okay, bud, it's time for us to go," Logan said as he looked down at the dog and then opened the back door of his car.

The dog cocked her head in question.

"We've got to take you to a rescue. Get you taken care of."

Logan motioned to the backseat, but the dog didn't move.

"Come on, it's okay," Logan said in a lighter tone.

Nothing happened.

"It's okay," he continued. "Look, I'll show you."

Logan crawled into the backseat. The dog hopped in right behind him and wagged her tail.

"Aw, hi bud," Logan said as the dog rubbed her face against his arm. "I guess you didn't need too much convincing after all, huh?"

The dog wiggled and pressed her body weight against Logan like they were long-lost friends.

"You're big on the cuddles, huh?" Logan asked as he laughed and continued petting the dog. "And a cute cuddler at that. How'd you get out here, anyway?"

CLOVER

I was riding in a car! I was riding in a car! I loved riding in cars. Scents swirl by at such a rapid pace in cars. It's like eating ten meals a second.

And this car did not disappoint. Not only were there massive amounts of appealing scents *outside*, but there were also intriguing scents *inside*. The car actually smelled a little bit like… chicken! It smelled like chicken. I used to chase chickens morning, noon, and night. Oh, how I missed the scent of chicken. Even the boy driving the car smelled like chicken! I never wanted to leave.

I hadn't trusted many people since I'd left home, but this boy was different. He looked at me with love in his eyes, he was calm, and he genuinely seemed kind. Plus, he smelled fantastic. I don't know where he'd come from to have such an intoxicating chicken scent attached to him, but I hoped that's where we were going.

"Hi, this is Logan Greenfield. I, uh… I found a stray dog and I was wondering if…" The boy paused. "Yes, okay, great. We'll be there in about… five minutes."

He paused again. I wondered who he was talking to. Was it me? I sat up to listen closer to his words.

"Yes, sounds good. See you soon."

The boy set his phone down, turned his head slightly toward me, and said, "All right, buddy, we're going to Kiwi Canine Rescue. The owner's expecting us in a few minutes."

I didn't understand what he was trying to tell me, but he spoke without any alarm in his voice. I sat tall and panted in agreement.

When the car stopped, the boy turned to me and uttered some more words, one of which was "stay." It had never been my favorite word, and if I didn't sense any immediate danger, I usually opted to ignore it.

As the boy exited the car, I sprang into the front seat and snuck out his door to stand next to him. He jumped a little, but didn't yell, so I figured I'd made the right choice. He must not have meant it when he'd said "stay," after all.

I followed the boy to the building, my nose actively working to take in any more of the chicken scent to no avail as we walked across the parking lot. Once inside, my nose was overcome with the scent of other dogs. I could hear them in the distance but couldn't see any.

The boy looked toward a woman sitting at a desk, so I did, too.

"Hi, uh, I called earlier about the stray?"

My attention snapped back to the boy. Did he just say "stay" again?

"Oh yes, you must be Logan?" the woman asked with a broad smile as she stepped out behind her desk to shake the boy's hand. "Hi. I'm Miranda. Owner and operator of Kiwi Canine Rescue," she continued before looking over at me. "Oh, well, hi there, aren't you just beautiful."

The woman's words were full of excitement. Were we going to play a game? I looked around for a ball or toy.

"He's a cute dog," the boy said as he scratched the top of my head. "And pretty funny, too. He didn't seem too sure about me at first, but he did jump right into my car and even followed me in here without a leash."

"Ah, I see. I think you've got a special one on your hands," the woman said as she looked me over.

Then she rubbed behind my ears. I loved when people did that.

"And," she continued, "I think I should probably let you know, she's actually a girl," the woman said as she chuckled and bent down to look me in the eye. "But, anyway, I'm so glad you called. Where did you say you found her again?" the woman asked as she looked up at the boy and continued scratching behind my left ear.

She'd found a good spot. My leg started to thump while I forgot about tennis balls and games.

"Oh, it was right outside McCorley's Pub, down on River Ave. I saw her eating from their trash can in the alley and figured she must be a stray."

"Yes, it certainly sounds that way," she said to the boy before turning back to me. "But oh, you're such a pretty girl. And so lucky that this young man found you."

I closed my eyes and continued to soak in the affection. Even though the chicken scent wasn't in this building, it wasn't a complete letdown.

LOGAN

"So, what happens now?" Logan asked Miranda.

"Well, first, I'll take her back to see if she has a micro-chip. If she does, it should tell me who she belongs to. If she doesn't, then I'll keep her here until she has a new home."

"Okay, great. Well, thank you for taking her," Logan said as he turned toward the door and started walking away. The dog started to follow.

"I see you made a quick friend. You're welcome to stay while I check on her microchip if you'd like."

"Oh, I should probably get going."

"Okay, it's up to you, but it will only take a minute. Let me go grab a leash. I'll be right back."

Logan leaned down to pet the dog.

"It looks like you're in good hands, bud."

The dog wagged her tail as Logan's hand repeatedly swept over the top of her head.

"All right. Let's see how you do with this, girl," Miranda said as she approached the dog with the leash.

The dog backed away and shrunk behind Logan.

"Okay, I wasn't sure how that was going to go," said Miranda, "but this isn't surprising behavior for a stray. It's hard to know how much interaction they've had with others when they get here. So, change of plans. Let's see if she'll follow you. We just have to head to that room right there behind my desk if you don't mind walking toward it."

Logan obliged while the dog followed behind.

"Impressive," said Miranda. "You sure you just met this dog?"

Logan laughed as Miranda checked for the dog's microchip.

"Well, it looks like this cutie might be staying here for a while," said Miranda. "I'm not seeing anything." She set her scanner down. "So," she said while looking at Logan, "any ideas for a name?"

"Oh, hmm." Logan paused. "Well, considering I found her enjoying an Irish restaurant's leftovers… maybe… Clover?"

"Ah, I love it!" exclaimed Miranda. "Very fitting for this lucky girl," she said as she ruffled the fur on Clover's head.

Logan stood straighter. He'd never named anything beyond his childhood toys before. He thought back to the paw print and clover charms on his mother's necklace and smiled.

"Hi, Clover," Logan said as he bent down to give her another scratch behind the ears. "I'm Logan."

CLOVER

The boy and the woman kept petting me while saying the word "clover." I'd never heard that word before, but if it meant being showered in affection, it could easily become a new favorite.

The boy's repetitive touch was soft and caring. I enjoyed sitting by his side.

I lost some of my excitement when the boy left. The woman placed a smooth, thin rope around my neck that tightened when I tried to pull, and she led me to another room. The room where the dog noises had been coming from.

There was a long hallway, and the floor was cold on my paws. The smell of all of the dogs together filled my nostrils as the woman showed me into what seemed to be a super clean closet with a barred door. The sides of the strange closet were solid and had a slight sheen that matched the floor.

"Okay, Clover," the woman said as she reached her hand through the barred door she'd just exited. "Welcome to your temporary home."

Home? I wasn't sure I wanted to go back home. *Is she going to take me there?* I didn't really want to go. I barked.

"Okay, then! You approve," said Miranda. "I'll come by later to check on you. Okay, Clover? I just have to finish up some paperwork, but then we'll get you outside before dinner."

Dinner! Now she was speaking my language. There wasn't much I loved more than dinner. Except maybe breakfast.

When the woman left, I immediately jumped up onto the cot in the corner to get off the cold floor. While the room and the closet were fairly bright, it wasn't from the sun like I was used to.

I was used to spending most of my time outside. Back at home on the farm, I would run with the chickens when the sun rose; devour a savory breakfast, which usually consisted of kibble covered by a few meat scraps from the house; nap next to my favorite tree by the cows; explore in the woods; then nap in the sun on the house's front steps until the farmer returned and fed me dinner. Dinner was similar to breakfast, except it usually included some crunchy, bland ingredients from the garden. They weren't always my favorite, but I appreciated the variety and effort.

I wondered if dinner would be the same here. It'd been several days since I'd had a dinner like the one I used to have on the farm. My stomach growled while I shivered and curled into as tight of a ball as I could on the cot. I decided to take a nap, hoping to dream about my next meal.

LOGAN

Logan sat outside at Lou's Pizza in downtown River Ridge on Sunday afternoon, waiting for Drew to meet him for lunch before his next shift at work.

"Hey, man," Drew said, almost out of breath, as he approached Logan at his table. "Sorry I'm late."

"All good," Logan replied as he stood to greet his friend with a quick handshake and a half hug. "How's it going?"

"Good. Just got hung up with my parents. I pretty much went through a full-blown interrogation just to have lunch with you," Drew said as he rolled his eyes and plopped into his seat.

"Ha, man, sounds rough," Logan feigned before sitting back down.

"It was. You're so lucky you can just do whatever you want," Drew said with a sigh.

"Yeah, true," Logan replied, but he didn't really agree. *Drew doesn't know how fortunate he is to have two parents who care about his whereabouts*, Logan thought.

The boys picked up their menus, even though they already knew what they were going to get.

"So," Drew said as he flipped the menu over, "I didn't hear back from you after you came across that stray dog yesterday. How'd that go?"

"Oh yeah, it went great, actually. Clover hopped into my backseat and followed me into the rescue and everything."

"Clover, huh? Was that the name on the collar?"

"Oh, no. I gave her the name while I was at the rescue. Considering I found her outside McCorley's."

"Ah, right. Nice. Glad things went okay."

"Yeah, I was actually thinking about stopping by there this morning to see how she's doing but didn't think I should."

"Oh, you should go," Drew said. "They probably need some extra help anyway. My parents said they're always looking for volunteers. Actually, did you hear who's going to start volunteering there?"

A waitress stopped at the boys' table before Logan could take a guess.

"Hi there, what can I get for you?" the waitress asked as she took out a pad of paper and a pen.

"We'll get a large pizza—half chicken, half supreme, please," said Drew without even a glance at Logan.

"Actually," Logan said to Drew, "can we get half meatball instead of the chicken? I'm kind of chickened out lately from work."

"Yeah, of course," replied the waitress. "Not a problem. Anything to drink?"

"I'll just have water," said Logan.

"I'll take a lemonade, please," said Drew. He looked toward Logan. "You sure you don't want anything? I'll pay."

"I'm good, thanks," said Logan through gritted teeth as he forced a smile before handing the menus to the waitress.

"Okay, I'll have the drinks out soon," the waitress said before walking back inside.

"So," Logan said, "who's going to be volunteering at the rescue?"

"Oh," Drew said before clearing his throat, "right. Kylie Stephens."

A lump grew in Logan's throat as he tried to hide his simultaneous anxiety and excitement upon hearing Kylie's name.

"It's all she's talked about before choir practice," Drew said. "I'm surprised you hadn't heard already."

"No, uh, that's news to me," Logan replied. "I'm sure she'll enjoy it."

"Oh, don't try to play it cool," Drew said. "We all know how hard you're crushing on her."

"I don't know what—" Logan started.

"Oh, come on. You get to school at what? 7:30? When your first class is a study hall, so you don't even *actually* have to show up until 8:50. And why? Why would you possibly do that?" Drew asked with an eye roll.

"I wake up early. So what? That's no reason to think—"

"Oh, I know what it could be," Drew said with his voice rising. "Maybe, *maybe* it's because 7:30 is when Kylie arrives for her morning meetings, and you might just have a shot at walking in with her.”

“Man, okay, keep it down,” Logan replied with wide eyes as he glanced at his surroundings. “I didn’t realize you were a professional private investigator, jeez. Who hired you anyway?”

“Her parents.”

Logan’s face lost some color.

“Dude, I’m just kidding. I mean, her parents and my parents are tight and all, but I’m pretty sure her parents don’t even know you exist. Actually, I’m pretty sure *Kylie* barely knows you exist.”

It could be true, Logan thought. He’d only moved to River Ridge a little over a year ago and hadn’t grown up with all the kids in their class like Drew had.

The waitress came back to the table with the boys’ drinks.

“Here you go,” she said as she placed the drinks in front of them. “One water and one lemonade. Is there anything else I can get you two for now?” she asked as she wiped her damp hands together.

“Actually,” Drew started, “we could use your opinion.”

Logan shrunk back into his seat as Drew continued.

“Say a guy has a crush on you…”

The waitress raised her eyebrows and took the slightest step back.

“Would you rather he makes it clear and asks you out, or would you rather he be super subtle and never tell you?”

"Dude, stop," Logan interjected as he sunk down farther in his chair.

"What? I just thought it would be nice to get a female's perspective on this, you know?" said Drew.

Logan shut his eyes, shielded his face with his hand, and prayed for the conversation to end.

"Oh, I would prefer if he told me," said the waitress definitively. "I am taken, though. Just to be clear," she said a bit slower.

"Oh," Drew replied with a reassuring smile. "Of course. No, it's nothing like that. I'm just trying to convince Logan over here to make his presence known with *his* crush."

"Ah, I see. Well, in that case, I would say go for it," said the waitress.

Logan caught her sympathetic look out of the corner of his eye.

"I'll be back in a few minutes with your food," she said with a smile before walking away.

Logan knew he had to step up his game if he was going to get on Kylie's radar, but he didn't want to push it. Logan hadn't dated anyone since he moved to town and Kylie was the only girl that had his attention. Maybe this school year would be the year he'd make a move.

CLOVER

After spending an entire night in my new cold closet and eating the same bland meal twice since I'd arrived, I was ready for something to change.

I'd already grown used to the sounds of the other dogs in the room. Even though I hadn't met them yet, I had a lot of them identified by their noises. There was the scared shrieker who would let out a high-pitched squeal-bark every time a door opened, the soft crier who whimpered when the lights went out for the night, the eager eater who, unless he was consuming food, barked the whole time someone was inside the room with kibble, and there was the heavy breather who stayed in the closet next to mine. He didn't move around much, so I wasn't sure why he was always panting. I could smell more dogs than I could hear, so I figured the others were just quiet types. Then there was me. I was the passionate adventurer, patiently waiting for someone to free me from my small closet for a day of fun on the run.

I heard the door open and smelled the woman from the previous day enter the room.

Wish granted. *I'm ready to go. Come and get me!*

The woman had another dog with her this time. I could hear the dog's nails tap hurriedly on the hard floor. They stopped in front of my door. I went up to sniff the other dog. She was about the same size as me, but petite for her type. I'd seen larger versions of her in my past. She was black with a short coat and a big smile. She sat down next to the woman and looked up at her. I jumped at my door for them to let me out. The woman said "down" in a stern voice, so I decided to sit and see if that would help things move along faster.

"Good girl," she said.

I always liked hearing the word "good."

"Clover, this is Kiwi, my dog. Kiwi, this is Clover."

Clover! I remembered that word from yesterday. *Please pet me again.*

"Clover, I think you'll like Kiwi. She's a Labrador Retriever and loves a good game of fetch. And, looking at you, I think you're a fetch-loving dog yourself. If I'm not mistaken, you're a Nova Scotia Duck Tolling Retriever. Maybe even a purebred. Ready to go out and play?"

Now she was talking. And she opened my closet door!

The woman petted me on the head and placed the smooth rope from yesterday around my neck. She asked me to sit, and I happily obliged. I could tell we were going somewhere fun!

The other dog remained outside of my space, and I was excited to meet her.

The woman brought me out of the closet, and I got to sniff my new dog friend. She didn't seem terribly interested in meeting me and maintained her focus on the woman.

"Miranda, are you in there?"

Miranda. I remembered that word from yesterday, too.

"Yes, back here with Kiwi and the new dog!"

"Oh, okay. I have someone calling about the next volunteer orientation. Is the next one this Saturday?"

"Yes, 9:00 a.m. And we could certainly use more volunteers."

"Thanks! I'll let them know."

The door shut and the stranger's scent subsided. My attention went back to the black dog. Her attention was on the fabric pouch that was strapped around the woman's waist. There must be something good in there.

"Come on, let's go, Clover. You're doing a great job so far."

We walked past my neighbor, the heavy breather, first. He was scruffy, larger than I expected, and light colored. He looked at us sleepily from his own cot in the corner. Eager eater was next to him barking his usual loud melody. Then we passed another small dog in the closet next to him. She was tiny and almost looked bald. I hadn't heard her from my room before.

I followed the dog and the woman outside to the large open area that was covered in both grass and dirt. I had been

taken out here to relieve myself, but I hadn't had the opportunity to explore quite yet. Maybe there was a way out.

"All right, girls, it's play time! Time to get rid of some
of that excess energy I know you both have."

The woman held up her hand, and the other dog sat
down. I sat too. The woman opened her mysterious waist
pouch, and I heard an excited whimper escape the dog. The
woman pulled out a ball!

The other dog and I were off as fast as we could go,
running after the bouncing glory that was this ball. It was so
fun being free again! The other dog snagged the ball off a
bounce and started running back to the woman. I decided to
keep running the other way and around the fence wall of the
enclosure. The wind felt nice blowing against my face, flying
by my ears, and gliding across my body. The sun was shining
bright and warming my cold, nature-neglected fur. I loved to
be outside!

"Come on, Clover!" I heard the women yell.

She sure said "clover" a lot.

I continued to run one way, then the other. At full speed,
my tongue draped happily out the side of my mouth in the
breeze. This, I knew, was pure joy. I ran back toward the
woman and the dog after a couple more laps. She had the ball
again!

The other dog and I sat down just like before, and the
woman threw the ball even farther this time and a bit closer
to my side. I ran straight for it and watched the other dog stare

at the ball as it entered my mouth. As we raced back, I felt like I could get used to this game, but my mind also started to drift each time I ran back to the woman. Would I be seeing the boy who smelled like chicken again? How long was I going to be staying here?

Then I was off again, racing after the coveted ball and relishing in the wind.

LOGAN

Logan shuffled his belongings around in the back of his car in his school's parking lot Monday morning at 7:31 a.m., trying to look busy while hoping Kylie would pull up any minute. Once he ran out of stalling tactics, he swung his worn, dark red backpack over his shoulders and grabbed a water bottle from his backseat before shutting the door. As he approached the school's entrance, he could see Kylie's car come barreling down the road, faster than usual.

He raised his arm up straight in a way that looked more like he had an eager question in class than a typical way of saying "hi" from a distance. As he watched her car pass by, he was unable to see through her windshield's reflection to see if she'd even noticed him.

Lame, Logan thought. *Lame, lame, lame. What was that? Why can't you just wave like a normal person?*

Logan continued to mentally beat himself up as he headed to his locker with his shoulders slumped.

He tried to reassure himself that he still had a shot at seeing Kylie before classes started. He wanted to tell her about Clover and the rescue. Maybe dogs could be their thing.

After fumbling with his locker combination, Logan opened the door on his third attempt. He grabbed his history and math books for his morning classes and shut the door.

And there was Kylie. The day was starting to look up.

"Hey! How's it going, Logan?"

She was so confident in her delivery. Was it a simple question? Yes. But Logan hadn't even talked to Kylie yet, and he already felt like the biggest failure in the hallway.

"Hey!" Logan shouted before lowering his surprisingly loud voice. "Hey, Kylie. I'm good. I uh…"

Kylie kept walking, but turned toward Logan, listening.

Logan continued. "Uh, how are you doing?"

"Good! It's nice to see you. I'll have to catch up with you later, okay? I've got to go see Mr. Apollo for some math help before our class later. I'm pretty sure I did not understand the last half of that assignment. I'll see you later!"

And then she was off. And Logan's straight arm wave was back. *Seriously, what is that*? he wondered.

Logan put "practice waving" on his mental to-do list for Monday evening, right after visiting Clover. After speaking with Drew on Sunday and making it through another shift at work, he decided he had to go visit Clover Monday after school. He hoped she was okay and wondered if she wanted to see a familiar face. Then again, maybe she'd already forgotten about him. But he was willing to give it a shot.

CLOVER

I was quite tired after the game of fetch with the other dog in the morning. I'm pretty sure her name was Kiwi. Every time the woman yelled out "Kiwi" she would come over to her. She'd continued to say "clover" to me. Did she think that was *my* name? I'd only ever been called Rain. Would she ever know that's my real name? "Clover" seemed clunky, and it took longer to say than "Rain." *Clover. Clover. Cloooover. Clover!* I continued to practice the name before I let myself drift off to sleep on my cot, stretched out on my back with my paws limp in the air.

I dreamt about being back on the farm, my old home, but it was dark and muddy. The rain was coming down hard, so I took shelter inside the old barn. The barn's doors were always open, so while it provided a fairly safe refuge during a storm, I wasn't typically the only animal that thought so. Sometimes the chickens would be in there, but they wouldn't stay long once they saw me. Other times there'd be squirrels chasing each other in the loose hay. On rare occasions, I'd even see one of those untrustworthy furry cats like I'd seen the other day in the alley.

There weren't any chickens or squirrels in the barn in my dream. To my surprise, there were little dogs! Six tiny orange dogs snuggled together in the back corner of the barn on their own little bed of hay. Then I saw my old family! I tried to bark, but no noise came out in my dream. I tried to run toward them, but I couldn't move no matter how hard I tried. I cried, but I was met with silence again. I watched as my old family scooped up one of the tiny dogs. I could hear them speaking.

"I wonder where these little guys came from," said Cheryl, the wife of the farmer.

Then the girl spoke. "Oh we *have* to keep them! Jake and I can each have three! We can take care of them and love them and feed them and walk them and play fetch with them and—"

"There's no way anyone is keeping anything I see in here," said the farmer.

Cheryl's eyes narrowed as she looked over to the farmer, then smiled. The farmer shrugged and walked back out into the rain.

"Come on, Gloria. Let's get these puppies inside and maybe, if we're lucky, we can keep *one*."

"Yes! We can keep one! I can't wait to tell Jake! Oh, oh, how about this one?!"

"Sure, yes, Gloria. That looks like a great choice. Now let's get inside before this rain gets worse," said Cheryl.

"Rain! Let's name her Rain," said Gloria.

I woke up upon hearing a whimper. Had that been *my* whimper? Gloria… my girl. The weather had changed so much since I'd last seen her.

"Miranda, are you in here?" someone asked from the doorway.

"Yes! In the back preparing some treats!" replied Miranda.

"Okay, I have someone named Logan on the phone? Wondering if he can stop by in a few minutes to visit with Clover?"

Are they talking about me? I would like to go outside again. Maybe the sun would help with the feeling I was left with after my dream.

"Oh, yes! Logan. He's the boy that found Clover. Of course he can come visit! I was just about to take some dogs outside. I'll make sure she's part of that group, and he can meet us out front."

"Okay, sounds good! I'll let him know."

The woman didn't have a ball with her when we went out this time, so I opted to lie down and let the sun warm my thick fur. While there were other dogs outside with me, I just wanted to be alone by the fence. I closed my eyes and thought about Gloria and the rain. And my previous farm life and the chickens. But then I caught a whiff of… what was that? It was faint. Could it be… chicken? I opened my eyes toward the direction of the scent. It was chicken! Here came the boy!

I could hear the boy yell, "Hi, Miranda! Hi, Clover!"

I stood up and looked at the boy with my tail wagging. His arm shot straight up like he was going to catch a rogue tennis ball. I watched as his stiff arm waved back and forth, almost like the wipers on a car's windshield. It didn't seem like an average human's greeting. *Is he trying to tell the woman that something's wrong with his car? Is it going to prevent me from riding in it again?*

Regardless of the boy's surprising arm motions, I was so excited to see him again. *Please pet me. You can call me Clover.*

LOGAN

Logan walked toward the enclosure where Miranda stood with the other dogs. Clover had been lying by herself, but Logan was relieved to see her stand with her tail wagging once she saw him.

"Here, come on in, Logan," said Miranda as she opened the fence door. "It's good to see you again!"

"You, too! And it's so good to see you, too, Clover," Logan said as he bent down to rub behind Clover's ears.

Clover rubbed against Logan while her tail continued to wag.

"She's such a sweet girl," said Miranda. "Definitely an independent girl, but she loves when people pet her."

"Yes, I think she's made that clear! I'm so glad she's doing well here. She's been on my mind a lot," said Logan.

"Well that's really sweet. Do you have any pets?"

"Oh, no. I wish. It's just me and my dad over off Route 3 in the Evergreen Trailer Park. I'm pretty sure pets aren't allowed, but even if they were, it wouldn't go over well with my father."

"Ah, I see. Well, Clover is one lucky gal to have you visit. You know, we actually have a volunteer program if you're interested in spending more time with the dogs. We could always use some extra help."

"Right, I've actually heard about that and thought about it. But, well, I'm not sure how helpful I'd be. I have school, my job…"

"Right, no pressure. We don't ask too much from our volunteers, but I understand if it doesn't work with your schedule. Our volunteers go through a one-day orientation that consists of a video; a tour; some hands-on work with my own dog, Kiwi; and finally a question-and-answer session. Our next orientation session is actually this coming Saturday. After orientation, we just ask that our volunteers commit to at least five hours of volunteer time per month. There's an online signup chart so people know what times are most needed, but it's pretty lax. Extra help is always appreciated."

"Oh, okay. Maybe I could make it work then. I really do like seeing Clover, and I'm sure the other dogs are great, too."

"Oh, yes. We've got a great group right now. We have nine here full time and a couple of others are being fostered right now. We don't have more than ten at a time at the rescue."

Logan stood but continued to pet Clover who contently remained at his side.

"Do they end up staying here long?" Logan asked.

"Ah, well, it just depends. We've had some older dogs that do typically end up staying for the remainder of their lives here, but I have some good foster parents who will usually take the older dogs. The younger and middle-aged dogs stay here anywhere between two weeks and two years, really. It just depends."

"Clover, here, will probably be a favorite," Logan said as he looked down at Clover. "I'm sure you won't be here too long, girl."

Clover nudged his arm for some more love.

"I'm sure she won't," said Miranda. "She will be here for at least two weeks, though. That's the time I require to monitor new dogs' behavior and get a better understanding of which home would be the best fit for them."

"Ah, did you hear that, Clover? I'll be seeing you for at least two weeks!"

Logan bent down to continue petting Clover face to face. Clover quickly licked his ear.

"Well," Logan continued, "I guess if that's all right with you, Miranda."

"Yes, of course. Does this mean you'll be joining us on Saturday?"

"Yes, I think so," said Logan as he stood back up. "I'll be there."

"Great to hear! We have a couple of others signed up for the class, but not as many as I'd hoped, so I'd love for you to join us. I think Clover would love it, too! Did you want to take a quick tour? I can have my husband, Ben, come out and watch the dogs while they wrap up their outdoor time. He's just inside finishing up some paperwork."

"Oh, thank you, but I should really get going. I have to clock in by 5:00."

Logan left the rescue after petting Clover on the head one last time to say goodbye. As he drove away, he realized how excited he was by the opportunity to volunteer at the rescue. Clover gave him the perfect reason to volunteer alongside Kylie. Ah, Kylie. Logan started smiling unknowingly while he stared at the upcoming stop sign. As the car came to a halt, so did his thoughts. He had to work on Saturday.

CLOVER

After coming back inside, I rested on the floor and looked out through the barred door of the closet. I'd learned to drown out the barking and whining that came from the others. I closed my eyes and thought about how fun it had been to see the boy again. He still smelled like chicken, and his touch exuded love. I hoped he could feel the same back from me. I missed him already. I wondered why he hadn't taken me with him. I had to think it was because something was wrong with his windshield wipers like he'd been trying to tell the woman. I figured he'd be back when his car was fixed. Then we could go out for another chicken-scented car ride and maybe explore in the woods after we had a tasty meal together.

The next morning was similar to the previous mornings in the cold space. The food was the same, the sounds were the same, the smells were the same. I longed for a bowl of food with some variety and flavor. I craved some warmth and juiciness to complement the crunch that was my new bland bowl of breakfast and dinner. Where were the meat scraps? Where was the fresh crunch from the garden? There must not be a farm close by.

I had come a long way from my previous farm, but I knew there were other farms out there. I was so far from my prior home that I wasn't sure I could get back to it even if I wanted to.

Once it had become just me and the farmer, day in and day out for weeks, I had lost hope, happiness, and purpose on the farm. I hadn't realized that when the rest of the family had left, that it was going to be forever, but I knew now. After witnessing the loudest yelling noises between Cheryl and the farmer, and after seeing how quickly she whisked away her children, I should have known they would never come back. After weeks alone with the farmer, I knew I had to go, too. Why stay somewhere when there's no love? There were no more scraps in my food at the farm, and no more crunch from the garden in my kibble. On my last two days on the farm, there wasn't even any kibble. I started to look at the chickens with more interest; but even though Gloria and the family weren't around to bear witness, they had loved those chickens, so I could never hurt one, no matter how hungry I was.

My final morning on the farm was kibble-less and love-less, and while the air continued to get warmer throughout the day, it still felt cold to me. I circled the fence that contained the chickens, stopped by the barn where I'd met the family, and walked one last time to the front porch. The farmer's truck was gone. No one was home, and I wouldn't be missed. My last sniffs at the farm brought in scents of hay, eggs, feathers, and growing grass. There were no more scents of Gloria,

Cheryl, Jake, and sweet morning breakfasts. The farm had grown sullen. I didn't want to grow sullen with it.

My first outing as a lone dog was exhilarating. I went behind one of the buildings that Cheryl would always stop at to connect a long, rancid smelling hose into her vehicle. I never understood why she did this. Others would come by and do the same. No one ever appeared to find it fun. With all of the things people could do, I didn't always understand why they wasted their time doing things that didn't make them happy.

As a runaway dog out on my own, I ran around to the back of the building on my first day out to get to the luring scents inside a plastic trash container. I tipped it over and was excited by the variety of edible pieces of discarded waste that I encountered. I savored each morsel of food and ate until my stomach hurt. Afterwards, I sauntered to a nearby river and threw up, then drank from the flowing stream. After resting for a few minutes in the sun, I was off again, feeling rejuvenated. Without a clear destination in mind, I still felt like I was headed in the right direction.

LOGAN

Logan's face scrunched as he heard his car's bumper crunch against the cement barrier at the end of his parking space in the back of River Ridge Chicken. He threw his car in park and made a mental note to back his car up slowly when he left for the night. He didn't usually park in the back, but sometimes on weeknight shifts he was able to snag a spot.

"Hey, man," said Seth as he exhaled smoke not far from Logan's car. "I didn't know you were working tonight. That new manager of ours really turned all of our schedules upside down, didn't he? I don't know why Bill felt he had to do that."

"Heh, yeah, tell me about it," Logan replied, thinking about how he'd need to get Saturday off. "How are things going tonight?"

"Not bad. Bill has actually only micromanaged about eighty percent of the things I've done so far tonight, so things may be looking up."

"Only eighty percent? Man, it must seem like a vacation in there. I wonder if it will go that well for me," said Logan.

"Oh, I have no doubt. You *are* Bill's favorite, after all. You do know that, right?"

"What? What makes you say that?"

"Dude, you can do no wrong! I get my wrist slapped if I take out the fries right when the buzzer goes off, like we're *supposed* to. But he's convinced that they need an extra five seconds for 'optimal fry-age,' whatever that means. You, on the other hand, could take those fries out while they're still frozen and he would make it the new protocol."

"Ha, well, let's go find out!" Logan said, playing along, but fixated on when the right opportunity would be to work on getting his schedule changed so he could attend the rescue's orientation on Saturday with Kylie.

An hour passed and Logan hadn't seen Bill. He was hoping to ask for his permission to change his schedule.

"Hey, Seth, do you think Bill already left for the night?" Logan asked while he refilled the chicken sandwich wrappers.

"Man, I don't know. If he did leave already, that would certainly be a first," replied Seth. "Yo, Sarah, is Bill's car still here?" Seth asked their fellow co-worker while she took her break at one of the tables in the dining area.

Sarah looked out the window from her table.

"Umm… I don't see it. He must've left. Maybe he actually got tired of hearing himself nag, too," Sarah said before taking a bite of her sandwich.

"Damn," said Logan.

"Man, do you like Bill as much as he likes you or something?" Seth joked. "Don't tell me you're upset he's not here. We're free! We can actually be efficient!" Seth exclaimed as he placed a pair of tongs in each of his hands to fish out two pieces of chicken from the fryer simultaneously.

"No, I just needed to work out a schedule change," replied Logan.

Sarah came closer to the counter while loudly slurping up the last few sips of her drink.

"You don't need Bill to change your schedule," said Sarah. "Out of the two years I've been here, I've never needed manager approval. And I've had over five managers while I've worked here. They never want to be bothered with stuff like that. They just want the employees to work it out them-selves."

"Okay…" said Logan, hesitant to believe her, but feeling like he had no other option. Kylie was more important than getting Bill's blessing for a change in workdays.

"What change are you needing?" Seth asked.

"I need to have Saturday off this week."

"Ah, yeah, I'm out," said Sarah. "Good luck with that!"

"Yeah, man, a Saturday? No one is going to want to take your Saturday," said Seth.

"Yeah, I know, I know. But I really need it off. You're on Sunday, right? I'll take your Sunday if you can take Satur-day."

"Ha, yeah, it's going to take more than that. Saturdays are the worst! I worked them for four months straight after I was hired. I'm done with that newbie schedule," replied Seth.

"I get it. I do. When else are you working? You must want *something* changed with your schedule?" Logan asked, still hopeful.

The back-and-forth of an attempted compromise lasted for another hour off and on as they continued to work before Seth's shift finally ended. In the end, Logan agreed to work both Friday night and Sunday, and he'd also wash Seth's car every week for the next month. Surely, it would've been easier if Bill had been there that night, Logan thought. But he was okay with the repercussions of the schedule change with Seth because he was going to be able to spend hours with Kylie on Saturday. Logan's previous uninterrupted time with Kylie was less than an hour, and that was only if he included time in class staring at the back of her head. This coming Saturday was going to be a huge breakthrough for Logan, and while he was thankful and relieved to now have the time off, he was starting to grow anxious.

Then he thought of Clover. He'd get to see Clover again on Saturday, too. He took a deep breath and began to think of Saturday with optimism and excitement as he pictured himself with Kylie and Clover together.

CLOVER

The next few days were a bit of a blur for me, but there were a few events that stood out to separate the days. The first day after I'd most recently seen the boy was cold and quiet. I could hear rain falling on the roof, and visitors left small wet puddles as they traipsed by.

I'd gotten to know some of the frequent visitors. They were mostly around when the woman wasn't. I'd come to learn that the woman's name was Miranda. Then there was her friend Cleo. Cleo liked to yell to Miranda while she stood in the doorway. She didn't come by my closet much, but she'd reach her hand in to pet me when she did walk by. There was also Ben. He seemed to be quite smitten with Miranda. He also didn't come into the dog room too often, but he was sweet and affectionate when he did.

Other visitors were a little more generous. There was a young man with short, light hair who would always slip me a flavorful treat. His smell reminded me of Gloria and Jake's grandma when she'd visited the farm. I'd seen him three times since I'd seen the boy last, and I devoured the tasty treats he offered each time. I don't think he was as generous with the other dogs.

Then there was the most active visitor, Zoe. She liked to take us all out on walks and out to the yard to play. She was tall, smelled like apples, and always wore the shoes that people had on when they were running.

There had also been a few visitors who hadn't come back. They'd stopped by briefly to see me but seemed more focused on the other dogs. Then yesterday, something weird happened. There were a couple of people who had come into the dog room along with Miranda and Ben. After walking around the room and visiting with all of us individually, they took my heavy-breathing neighbor outside with them. And then he didn't come back. Not even at night. I wasn't sure what happened to him, and I wasn't sure if it was good. Did he run away to eat out of trash containers? I had a hard time picturing it. He really hadn't done a whole lot of moving around since I'd arrived. Did he get lost and was stuck outside now? That was hard for me to imagine, too. Surely, someone would've heard him breathing and led him back to his closet. Did he have to leave because he was too loud? I started to wonder how loud I breathed. But that didn't make sense, either. There were dogs louder than the heavy breather.

The next day, Zoe came over along with Miranda and her dog, Kiwi.

"Time for a stroll!" exclaimed Zoe. She was always so cheerful. It was a nice contrast to my current living quarters.

"She's just the cutest, isn't she?" Zoe asked Miranda as she entered my space to slip the smooth rope around my neck to go outside. "It probably won't be long before someone decides to adopt her, huh?"

"Yeah, I think she'll go pretty fast," replied Miranda.

"I'm sure you'll end up in the best home, Clover," said Zoe. "And until then, I'm excited to hang out with you. Now, let's get walking."

The walk was exactly what I needed. I started to feel my sense of adventure seep back into my bones and radiate through my muscles as I walked alongside Zoe, Kiwi, and Miranda in the woods. Inside, I was becoming drained, even depressed. I had trouble finding excitement in each day while inside the dog room and stuck in my closet.

I embraced every minute of that walk. The air was turning crisper, and there were more and more leaves on the ground each time I went outside. As we walked on the trail, I tried to catch a falling leaf in my mouth, hoping they'd be more flavorful than the last time I'd tried eating one. Maybe if I caught one that was fresh off a tree, it would taste better than the ones that had already landed on the ground. A few minutes later, I was disappointed to find out that wasn't actually the case.

"So," said Zoe, "are you feeling ready for tomorrow's orientation?"

"Oh, yes," said Miranda, "I do believe so. We have close to ten people signed up now, and there are even a couple of younger folks who will be part of the group. Two from River

Ridge High. I'm sure the dogs will enjoy their company. Actually, one of them is the boy who brought Clover to us."

I looked over to Miranda expectantly at the sound of my new name. Did she need me to stop? She was still walking. Did she have a treat? I didn't smell anything. Was this about the leaf? I didn't even enjoy it.

"Oh that's great!" exclaimed Zoe. "I'm sure she'll be so excited to see him. Sounds like a nice boy."

"Yes, he is. His name is Logan."

Logan! I'd only ever heard this word when the boy was around and started to wonder if that was his name. Was he going to stop by today? I hadn't seen him for days. It must be his car problem. It was probably hard to fix windshield wipers. Hopefully he'd get them taken care of and I'd see him again soon.

LOGAN

One more day, one more day, Logan repeated to himself as he drove to school on Friday. He started to make a mental list of things he could talk to Kylie about tomorrow at the rescue. He'd compliment her, ask about volunteering, and if she had a dog…

Logan stopped working on his list as he pulled up next to Kylie's car in the school parking lot. After not walking in with her all week, there she was. He felt his heartbeat quicken. He was excited to see her, but he also felt unprepared since he'd been so focused on Saturday.

Kylie had just finished gathering her things when Logan parked his car. She waited by her car and waved. Logan picked his hand up from his steering wheel for a quick wave back, relieved he didn't have enough space in his car to live out another awkward wave moment.

"Hi, Logan!" Kylie said as Logan stepped out of his car.

"Kylie! Hi! How are you?" Logan said with a big smile before grabbing his belongings from his backseat.

"I'm good, thanks. How about you?"

"Oh, fine, fine. Thanks," Logan said as they began walking toward the school together. "You look really nice today."

"Really? That's sweet. It's just jeans and an old t-shirt. I don't usually put much thought into my outfits come Friday."

Kylie could make anything look amazing, Logan thought. He didn't see just jeans and a t-shirt. He saw a green top that made her eyes pop, jewelry that expressed her creativity without being excessive, and jeans that no one else could make look so good.

"Ha, that's how I feel about every day I put my clothes together," Logan replied.

"Well, in that case, you don't do a bad job, yourself."

Logan tried not to blush. He also had on jeans and a t-shirt, but his jeans were old and the holes in them weren't about making a fashion statement, they were simply from wear and tear, and he couldn't imagine that the grey shirt he had on had any positive affect on his features.

"Ha, thanks," Logan replied. "So, I heard you were going to start volunteering at Kiwi Canine Rescue."

"Yes! Oh my gosh, I'm so excited. Orientation is tomorrow. I can't wait!"

"Same! I'm actually going to start volunteering there, too," Logan said.

He tried to make eye contact at appropriate times after realizing he'd been mindlessly staring down at the book he was carrying since they'd started walking together.

"You are?" asked Kylie. "That's great! So you'll be there tomorrow, too?"

"Yeah, it was kind of a last-minute decision, but I'm definitely looking forward to it. What made you decide to volunteer?"

"Oh, it was an easy decision and a long time coming. My parents wouldn't let me volunteer until I turned sixteen, so now there are no more excuses. We've never had a dog, so I have to volunteer to prove that I'm knowledgeable and responsible enough to adopt one."

"Aha, I see. So you'll be able to get a dog soon then, hopefully."

"Yes, that's the plan. I can't wait. What about you? Do you have any pets?"

"No, not right now, at least. I would love to have a dog, but I'll most likely have to wait until I'm living on my own in a couple of years."

"Ah, that's a bummer. I can't imagine waiting any longer for a dog. So are you volunteering for college applications then? Or are you just a dog lover?"

"Yeah, I'm not so sure about college, at least not right now, so I guess it's more to just be around the dogs," Logan replied. *And you*, he thought.

"Well, that's impressive," Kylie replied as Logan held the front door open for her. "It's not often you hear of high schoolers volunteering without an ulterior motive."

"Ha, yeah, I guess so." Logan replied.

Kylie turned to Logan while clutching her books tight in her arms. "I've got to run to a meeting, but it was so good catching up with you," Kylie said. "And now I'm even more excited about tomorrow."

"Same," Logan replied as he wracked his brain for more words, but ultimately came up with nothing.

"I'll see you later," Kylie said after a pause from Logan.

"Yes, see you later."

While Logan felt fairly confident about the conversation he'd just had with Kylie, he also realized that he'd just used up all of the conversation points that he'd come up with for the following day. Then Logan thought of Clover. Surely, Clover would give them plenty to talk about.

CLOVER

I woke up the next morning and jumped out of my cot for my morning shake. I'd grown used to the lack of jingle when I shook each morning.

While nothing looked different this morning, I felt more hopeful than I'd been since being here. Maybe today would be different. Maybe I'd be able to go out on another adventure, or for a car ride, or even get to see Logan again. I could see the sun's rays hitting the hallway floor by the door that led to the grassy area. I whimpered out of excitement and also a need to get outside.

A few moments later, I heard the door squeak open. The shrieker sent off his usual alarm, the barker chimed in with his usual tune, and I cried a little since I could smell Miranda *and* the boy who fed me treats. Was I going to get a treat before breakfast? I wagged my tail with anticipation.

Miranda came to my closet to retrieve me and take me outside to relieve myself. The air was even cooler than the day before, and the grassy area was partially covered by damp leaves. I took in the scents of wet grass and fallen leaves before I was brought back inside.

"How's Clover doing this morning?" the treat-giving boy asked Miranda while he fed me my breakfast in my closet. I could smell treats on him but was disappointed to find that there weren't any in my food bowl.

"She seems to be doing really great this morning," Miranda replied. "I actually haven't seen her have quite this much pep in the morning since she's been here."

Miranda looked down at me from outside my closet door.

"Do you know that today's going to be an exciting day, girl?" she asked. "Is that what's going on with you?"

"Are you excited for orientation, Clover?" treat-boy asked.

I wagged my tail upon hearing my name.

"Tim," Miranda began, "can you help me bring the stacks of chairs from the back closet into the training room this morning? I'd like to have twenty chairs set up in front of the TV and a few placed around the room for any volunteers that may pop in and out."

"Yes, not a problem. I'll have that all set up shortly. I can't wait to have some more volunteers around here. We've been pretty short-handed lately," he said.

Miranda sighed. "Right, yes," she said. "That can happen from time to time. We should get some good ones out of this upcoming group. I think it will be a great day."

I stuck my nose through the bars in my door to try to get Miranda's attention. It seemed like she was also having a good morning. Maybe something exciting really was going to be happening today. I was ready.

LOGAN

"Where are you off to?" Logan's dad, Dave, asked his son Saturday morning. "It's too early for work, isn't it?"

Logan inhaled, readying himself to reply quickly and then take off.

"Work meeting. I'll see you tonight."

Both statements were a lie. He was headed to Kiwi Canine Rescue, and he knew his dad wouldn't be home in the evening in time to see Logan again that day.

Logan didn't receive a reply from Dave before he left the house. He was surprised his father had piped up at all from his seat in the living room. He usually didn't bother talking to Logan, never mind question his plans. He must not be too hung over this morning, Logan figured. His father had been an alcoholic all of Logan's life and Logan was convinced that he'd never even wanted to have a kid. If Logan had never wanted a kid, then had one and had become the sole caretaker, he guessed he'd be miserable, too. At least that's what he told himself.

Whenever Dave was actually home, he was typically passed out in his living room chair or his bedroom if he made it that far, and Logan always attempted to avoid him. If Dave wasn't home, it meant that he was either working at the auto-body shop in the next town over or spending time at the bar next to the shop. If there was a trailer park closer to his father's workplace and favorite bar, they'd surely live there instead. But then again, moving their belongings to a new location would involve both change and effort and those were two things that did not jive well with his father.

As Logan got into his car, he couldn't help but smile. He could sense that he was inching closer to his goal of being with Kylie. He was also excited at the thought of spending more time with Clover and the other dogs at the rescue. He felt for these dogs that were shaped by a mysterious past, confronted with sudden change, and ultimately left without a family. Clover deserved to be a part of a family. He wished it could be his.

Logan glanced at the time on his car's dashboard. It was 8:58. The orientation was scheduled to start at 9:00 and he was at least five minutes away from the rescue. Logan had had plenty of time to get ready and out the door in time, but he'd filled his morning with chores to keep from growing too anxious about the upcoming day. While he was still excited, he knew he could've easily worked himself up and potentially opted out of going at all. He had to distract himself by keep-ing busy. He'd organized his bedroom, which hadn't been that messy to begin with, and then cleaned their one bathroom. Afterwards, he decided to make himself some pancakes. The colder weather made him crave maple syrup, and while the bottle of it that was pushed to the back of the fridge was potentially a year or two past any sort of "best used by" date, it tasted fine to him.

When Logan entered the orientation room, the first thing he noticed was the back of Kylie's head. A sight that he'd grown used to seeing in math class. She turned around and waved to him. Miranda was busy setting up a television at the front of the room with a couple of others. There was also a black lab in the room that stayed by Miranda.

"Logan, hi. I'm so happy to see you!" said Kylie. "For a second, I thought you weren't going to show! Here, I saved you a seat. You haven't missed anything."

"Hey, Kylie. It's good to see you, too," Logan said while slightly out of breath from rushing into the building with the thought that he was going to interrupt the group upon entering. "I really thought I was going to be late. Thanks for saving me a seat." He sat down next to Kylie, feeling slightly more at ease, yet even more nervous, at the same time.

"Me, too. Here, I snagged you one of the orientation folders. They're going to go through these after we watch a video," said Kylie.

"Oh, thank you," replied Logan. "Who's that cute black lab?"

"Oh, I think that's the owners' dog," said Kylie. "I'm pretty sure it must be Kiwi, the dog who the rescue is named after."

With the sound of her name, the black lab looked up and then trotted happily over to Kylie and Logan.

"Looks like you're right!" said Logan. "Hi, girl. You're so sweet," he said to Kiwi as the dog paced between the pair and nudged their hands.

"You're a real big dog lover, huh?" asked Kylie as she petted Kiwi.

"I guess I am! I actually brought a dog here the other day. I found her outside McCorley's after work. Her name is Clover," Logan said as he continued to pet Kiwi with Kylie. "She's one of the reasons I decided to volunteer."

"Oh wow! I didn't know that. That's so sweet! I'd love to meet her. What kind of dog is she?"

"I think she's a Nova Scotia Duck Tolling Retriever. Or a 'toller' for short, I've learned."

"Oh, sounds fancy! I don't think I've heard of that breed before," said Kylie.

"I hadn't either. She's medium-sized with lots of orange-ish fur and some white markings."

"Aw, she sounds cute."

"She is. I hope you get to meet her today."

"Yeah, maybe she'll even be the dog I get to adopt! How cool would that be? Although I'm sure it won't happen that quickly for me."

Logan loved this idea. Why hadn't that crossed his mind before? He wanted Clover to go to a loving home and it certainly couldn't be his. Why couldn't it be Kylie's?

"All right, everyone," said Miranda. "It's time to get started. Thank you all for coming this morning. We're all very excited to have you here for our volunteer orientation and training. My husband, Ben, and I started this rescue over a decade ago now, and we're always thankful when we have a new group of interested volunteers to support our mission of helping dogs in our community."

Logan smiled as he thought about finding Clover.

"We'll be starting with a brief video so that you can learn more about the history of the rescue and our procedures here. Then we'll go on a tour of the facility, watch some of our current volunteers demonstrate proper dog training here at the rescue, and we'll wrap up our day with time for questions and an opportunity to visit with some of our current canine residents."

After the video ended, Miranda went back to the front of the room.

"All right everyone, I hope you enjoyed the intro video. This place is truly my pride and joy, and I'm fortunate to call it home with Ben and my girl, Kiwi, here. Now, who's ready to check this place out?"

Logan was looking forward to getting up and walking around. He hadn't been sure what to do with his hands while sitting next to Kylie, and his palms had grown sweaty. Kylie had seemed so attentive during the video and not nervous at all. He wondered if her calm demeanor meant she was simply super self-assured or just not into him.

CLOVER

I jumped up at the sound of the dog room door opening. I'd been sprawled out on the floor catching my breath after a fun game of fetch in the yard with some of the other dogs.

I went to my barred door and wagged my tail upon hearing so many voices enter the room. For a second, I thought I could even hear Logan! And then I smelled him! It *was* Logan! I could hear Miranda talking to all of the people who had entered the room with her, but I was too excited to listen to any of her words. Logan!

Miranda and the people moved closer to my room, and I could see Logan in the group now. Did he bring all of his friends to play? They couldn't have all fit into his car, could they? Would there still be room for me?

He must not have seen me. I barked to get his attention, then he came over to me, along with Miranda and another girl who had been standing next to him.

"Ah, it looks like someone is excited to see you again, Logan!" said Miranda.

I whined until he finally stuck his hand through the bars in my door. *I missed you! You smell even better than before!*

I licked Logan's hands and tasted something familiar. It was the same sweet sauce that used to drift out from my previous family's windows some mornings. They would douse their breakfast plates with this sticky goodness, and I always considered myself lucky when Gloria would let me lick her fingers after her long breakfast mornings.

Chicken *and* sweet breakfast scents? Logan couldn't get much better.

"Hey, Clover," Logan said as he laughed and continued to let me lick his hands.

Yes? Please say my name again.

"It's good to see you, girl," he continued. "It looks like you're doing well! I want you to meet Kylie. Kylie, this is Clover. Clover, Kylie."

Clover Kylie? I hoped my name wasn't getting more complicated. I'd just gotten used to Clover.

The girl smelled different than Logan, but I still liked her. I watched as Logan's attention shifted to the girl as she petted me. She smelled a bit like flowers and... something sweet. Maybe it was blueberry muffins. I couldn't quite figure it out yet, but she mostly smelled like flowers. There were more edible scents on Logan. Was he going to pet me again?

"So, everyone," said Miranda, "I wanted to make sure you saw this piece of art. It provides a reminder about what volunteering here at the rescue is all about."

I watched as Miranda pointed to the picture hanging high on the wall outside my room.

"This artwork is an imprint of my dog, Kiwi's, nose print. Just like people all have unique fingerprints, a dog's nose print is actually unique to them. No two dogs are truly one hundred percent alike. I like to think that part of our purpose as individuals is to identify our own uniqueness and share it with the world in some capacity. And, as volunteers at the rescue, it's our job to help recognize and understand each dog's unique identity and abilities, then use them to help these dogs find their new forever home. These dogs have experienced trauma of some sort to end up here. So while we do our best to make sure they find their new homes, it's our responsibility to ensure they feel secure and loved as much, and as often, as possible while they're here."

I watched as Logan nodded along, seemingly listening to the words Miranda was saying, but also clearly distracted by the girl beside him. Was he trying to figure out what she smelled like, too? I wondered if he had a different idea than blueberry muffins. Would he tell me later? The girl, meanwhile, seemed to be locked in on what Miranda was saying. If there was going to be a test afterwards, Logan might need to go to her for some assistance. It was fun to be around both Logan and Miranda, but I wasn't sure what they were doing with this group. I hoped it resulted in play time, and soon.

LOGAN

After a demonstration on how to approach, leash, and walk a dog, it was close to 11:00 a.m. and time for a break in the orientation room.

Miranda and the two other volunteers assisting for the day had laid out a spread of assorted mini muffins, orange juice, tea, and coffee.

Normally, Logan's stomach would be growling and ready for lunch around this time, but his large out-of-the-norm breakfast still had him feeling full. He sat next to Kylie again who was busy flipping through her orientation folder.

"Would you like something to drink?" Logan asked Kylie. "I'm going to go grab a cup of orange juice."

Kylie looked up at Logan and grinned. He was in awe at how easily she smiled.

"Some orange juice would be great. Thank you."

Was his face turning red? It felt like his face was turning red. It was only a question about *orange juice. Get it together,* Logan thought.

"Hey, Logan, what do you think so far?" Miranda asked as he approached the refreshment table.

"Oh, this is great," Logan replied. "I can't wait to actually start volunteering,"

"I'm happy to hear that. And I think Clover was happy to see you again, huh? Make sure to visit with her again before you leave today if you have time. And bring your… friend?"

"Oh, Kylie? Yeah, she's just a friend."

"I see," said Miranda with a smirk. "Well, you and Kylie should definitely visit with Clover after the orientation is over. I know it'd mean the world to her. While it seems like she's starting to enjoy herself more here, you can tell she's a free spirit, so I think she's having a hard time being cooped up. And she adores you. I'm sure she'll adore your friend just as much."

Logan nodded. He was sure, too. Clover would probably even like Kylie more than him once she got to know her. How could she not?

Logan carefully held a cup of orange juice in each hand as he made his way back to Kylie, trying not to make a fool of himself by spilling the juice on the floor or himself. While Logan had experience working at a restaurant, it didn't involve delivering uncovered beverages to his one-and-only crush.

"One fresh orange juice, madam," said Logan as he slowly lowered her drink to ensure successful, spill-free delivery.

Kylie giggled. "Why thank you, sir. How kind."

The pair sipped their drinks while Logan stared down at his shoes and Kylie fiddled with her orientation folder.

"So," said Kylie, "are you having fun? I feel like I've learned so much already."

"Yes, same!" Logan said.

It was partially true. He'd certainly already learned some new things, but he was fairly confident that he'd need to read through the orientation folder on his own later to catch up on what he'd distractedly missed throughout the morning.

"It's just so energizing to be here and think about how we can positively impact these dogs' lives," said Kylie. "I can't wait to actually start volunteering and spending more time with them."

"I know, same," Logan said to Kylie. *And I also can't wait to spend more time with you.*

CLOVER

It'd been quiet since the group left. Well, quiet for the dog room, that is. There were the usual barks, cries, and whimpers that filled any potential moments of silence. I wondered if the heavy breather would ever be back.

I sat up as I heard the door open. Could it be the heavy breather? What an unusual and surprising day it was turning out to be if that were the case.

It wasn't. I heard Miranda and Logan, and I could smell chicken, flowers, and… maybe it was cookies. While Logan's food-heavy scents were a favorite of mine, the smell of food mixed with the outdoors had to be the second best. My intrigue for the new girl was growing.

I stood and wagged my tail as my mouth dropped open a little. I couldn't help but grin as the group approached. *Hey, Logan! Hey, Flower Cookies!* My body wiggled.

"It looks like she's warming up to you already," Logan said as he smiled at me through the barred door before looking over at the girl.

"It sure does," said Miranda. "Let's get a leash on her and take her out. I'm sure she'd just love to play fetch with you both."

I barked. I couldn't contain my excitement. Miranda had said "fetch"! I ran around in a circle and whimpered. Were we all going to play fetch together? This could easily be turning into one of the best days since my family was together with me on the farm.

When we got outside, I noticed some other dogs and people playing together, but I tuned them out as I zoned in on the ball in Logan's hand. Miranda left to talk to some of the other people outside, but Flower Cookies remained at Logan's side, smiling. She didn't have a ball in her hand, so my attention went back to Logan.

I ran up to him and licked his hand. *I'm ready!*

"Sit," said Logan.

I obeyed.

And then we were off! The ball and I soared across the grass. I was excited to see what it would taste like. I snagged it on its second bounce and circled straight back to Logan and the girl. They were both cheering me on. I dropped the ball in front of Logan's feet and was surprised when the girl grabbed it. I sat, still hopeful, and cocked my head to the right.

Then she threw it! I scooped it up with some blades of grass. Grass wasn't my favorite thing to eat. I'd only ever had it a few times, but I could accept a couple of pieces if it was part of playing fetch here.

I dropped the ball in front of Logan's feet again.

The girl giggled. "I think you're clearly her favorite."

"Well, I did rescue her I guess, so… it probably has something to do with that."

Logan laughed as he picked up the ball and threw it even farther than before. I loved how unpredictable this game was getting.

When I returned, Logan and the girl were standing closer together. I dropped the ball between them.

"Aha!" she said. "How quickly things change. Maybe we're on an even playing field now?"

"Maybe. Let's see what she does next, Kylie."

Kylie. They'd said this earlier. They didn't say "Clover" with it this time, but I still sat down and waited for what was next.

I continued to play and watch Logan and the girl move closer together with each throw. Maybe they enjoyed each other's scents, too. They were certainly smiling a lot. I was smiling, too, as I opted to lie down beside them in the sun as they continued to stand.

"Looks like she's pretty tuckered out! I'd say we did a good job," Logan said.

"Yes, I think so! How're you feeling, Clover? Did you have fun, girl?" the girl asked as she reached down to pet me and scratch behind my ears.

She had called me Clover. I liked how her voice sounded as she said my new name. It was soft and sweet. I also loved how much she was petting me. I rolled over so she could move onto my tummy. Then Logan bent down and started petting me, too. I closed my eyes as my paws went limp while I took in all of the belly rub sensations. I was loving being with Logan and this new girl.

LOGAN

"Aw, would you look at that," said Miranda as she sauntered over to Logan and Kylie showering Clover with love. "I think you two are easily Clover's favorite pair. She's so lucky to have you as volunteers now! Do you both know when you'll be back?"

"Yes!" Kylie exclaimed as she rose to her feet. "I plan on coming here at least a couple of times a week after school. Then also on weekends as much as I can. I can't wait to officially start. I should be here on Tuesday."

"Oh, that's great," replied Miranda. "So Clover will be seeing you again in just a couple of days! That's wonderful. How about you, Logan?"

"Um, well, definitely some point next weekend. My work schedule is a little unpredictable right now, but I'm hoping to come here after school sometimes as well."

"Okay, that sounds good. We do have our volunteer schedule online where you can sign up for vacancies, but you're always welcome to pop in any time that we're open, too, even if it's just for a few minutes. That's never a problem."

"Okay, great. Thanks, Miranda," Logan said as he took a break from petting Clover to stand up. Clover continued to sit between Logan and Kylie with her eyes slightly closed and a smile on her face.

"Hey, actually," Miranda started, "the Langfield fair is coming up next weekend. I usually have a few volunteers come along with a couple of the dogs to help get the word out about our mission and the dogs that are available for adoption. Would something like that interest either of you?"

"Oh, yes! I love the fair! That would be so fun!" Kylie exclaimed before turning to Logan. "Would you be able to come, too?"

"Yes. I, uh, think so," Logan replied. His mind was whirring from the potential of spending another day with Kylie that he couldn't even remember if he was scheduled to work or not. But more time with Kylie? How could he give that up? "I can make it work, I'm sure," he said while urging his voice to sound more confident.

"Oh that's just wonderful," Miranda said as she smiled and held her hands together like she was accepting applause. "We usually meet here in the morning around 9:00 or so, gather up the dogs and supplies we need, then head over to the fair as a group. We're usually there until about 3:00 or 4:00, then we come back here to unload. So it's a pretty big commitment; but even if you're able to help for just part of the day, it would be really helpful. And I promise you we have a ton of fun on fair days."

"That sounds great!" Kylie said as she smiled and glanced at Logan.

"Definitely. I can't wait," said Logan. "I should probably get going, though," he continued as he looked down at Clover. "But it was so good to see you again, Clover! You're just the best, aren't you?"

Logan bent down to Clover's level as she stood and faced him. He scratched behind her ears as he finished his goodbye and then turned to Miranda.

"Thank you so much for everything today. This was even better than I expected."

"Oh good, I'm so glad. We're happy to have you both," Miranda replied. "I'm going to go gather up some dogs and get them back inside. I can't wait to see you both again soon! Thanks for coming today."

"So, I guess I'll see you Monday?" Logan asked Kylie while briefly making eye contact.

Clover looked up expectantly at Kylie.

"Yes, hopefully I'll see you at the parking lot!"

Maybe Drew was wrong, and Logan was actually someone that Kylie noticed. Or was she just being nice?

"Yes, sounds like a plan!" Logan said, kicking himself for sounding overeager. He had to get out of there before he could say anything else.

As Logan walked toward his car, he started to wonder if he was actually capable of spending another day with Kylie. All he wanted was to spend more time with her, but he was starting to think avoiding her could be a safer option. If she wasn't interested in him, he'd never have to find out if they were never around each other. But what happened to this year being the year he'd give this a shot?

While driving home, Logan envisioned the cartoons that depict the angel and devil on each shoulder, but they were mini-Clovers. On his left side, Clover was lying down, withdrawn and sighing, wondering if Logan could handle pursuing a relationship with this girl. That Clover didn't think it was worth it to bother finding out. The Clover on Logan's right side was the happy Clover he'd just left, loving life and enjoying being around people. Happy Clover knew Logan could push through if he wanted to and, hey, maybe Kylie even liked Logan, too. The thought made Logan smile.

CLOVER

I was sad when Logan left, but the girl stayed a little longer and continued to scratch behind my ears. She seemed sad when Logan left, too. Her bright smile had faded slightly since he'd taken off. Maybe she loved to be around him, too.

"Well, girl, I think it's time for me to say goodbye. It was so good getting to meet you, Clover." The girl knelt down, and I softly nudged her head. "You're such a sweet, sweet girl. I'm so glad Logan found you." The girl rose to her feet but continued to look at me. "I'll see you soon, okay?"

The girl's shoulders slumped, and I watched as her smile faded even more as she stopped petting me before walking away. It saddened me to see her go, but I felt hopeful that I'd see her and Logan again. People like to do what makes them happy.

I walked over to Miranda to let her know I was without my people now. She let me inside, and I slept on my cot in the closet. It didn't seem quite as cold as it had been inside, but I still wasn't impressed with the food they kept dishing out. I hoped to wake up from my nap to the treat boy that smelled like Gloria and Jake's grandma. Ah, Gloria and Jake.

I tried to picture the last time I'd seen them and wondered where they were now. They had to be far away.

I woke up to Miranda's voice in the dog room. "Yes, right this way, we have so many great dogs right now. Are you looking for anything in particular?"

"I'm really not sure. My wife doesn't even know I'm here, but she's been talking nonstop about adopting a dog soon. And it's all I hear from my kids. I'm not quite on board yet, so I just wanted to look around and meet some potential candidates on my own so I could get more used to the idea."

"Ah, I see. Well, you've come to the right place. Let me introduce you to the few that are inside right now."

Miranda was stopping at each closet while talking to a mystery man. When she got to my door, I continued to lie down, understanding we weren't about to play a game.

"This, here, is our newest resident, Clover."

"Oh, he's pretty cute."

"Yes, *she*, actually, is really quite adorable."

"How're you doing, fella?"

I guessed he was talking to me. I wasn't all that intrigued by his empty hand, but I still walked over to the barred door.

"How old is she?" the man asked.

"We're guessing she's between two and three. She's such a sweet girl. She's taken to a few of our new volunteers already."

"I see. Well, this has been very helpful, thank you. It will probably be a few months before we decide to adopt a dog, but I'm glad I visited."

The man seemed unsure as he petted me. His touch didn't exude love as he stroked the top of my head. I looked over to Miranda for reassurance. Was this one of her friends? He didn't smell like a dog. He smelled more like leather and peppermint. Nothing I was drawn to. I didn't feel sad when he left.

Miranda slipped me a treat when the man was done standing at my door. She didn't hand out treats often, so it tasted extra good.

When Miranda left, I went back to my cot and sighed. Was I always going to be here?

LOGAN

"Hey, man, Earth to Logan…" Logan's co-worker, Steve, said as he waved his hand in front of Logan's face.

Logan opened his eyes a little more and tried to focus on the oven. He hadn't realized he was completely spacing out until Steve had spoken up. Steve was a longtime employee at River Ridge Chicken. Logan had always been in awe of how he actually seemed to enjoy working behind a fast-food counter, ensuring orders were completed correctly and as fast as possible. Steve was always on top of his game at work and unfortunately for others, he expected the same from everyone else one hundred percent of the time.

"Oh, hey, yeah, sorry."

"Are you going to let all the food burn today or what? We've got stuff to prepare. Get with it!"

"Yeah, sorry, Steve. I'll have the next two orders ready in a second."

It was no surprise that Logan's mind had wandered off this Sunday afternoon. The previous day had been filled with Kylie and Clover. He had a lot to recap, a lot to plan, and a lot to wonder about. *How was the fair going to go with Kylie?*

How was Clover doing? What was Kylie thinking today? What could he say to Kylie next? How long was Clover going to be at the rescue? Would she be adopted soon? Did he want her to get adopted yet? Did Kylie have a shot at getting Clover?

Logan had never felt so connected to a dog before, granted he'd never really had the chance. Clover made Logan feel happy, helpful, and if he really thought about it, loved. And Clover's actions around Logan made it seem like she felt happy and loved by Logan, too. He didn't want to lose her.

The next day on Logan's walk into school with Kylie, he decided to bring Clover up to her again to gauge her interest.

"Hey, so... I was thinking about Clover last night. She's such a great dog..."

"Oh, yes, she really is, isn't she? She's just the cutest. And sweetest. She seems to really love you. I'm so glad you found her."

"Same. She seems to really love you, too... so, I was thinking... I know we were kind of joking when we were talking about it before, but do you think maybe you really would be able to adopt her?"

"Oh. I really don't think I'm going to be able to adopt any time soon. My parents, well, my dad, really, has been really strict about this. I don't think a few days of volunteering are going to convince him that we're ready for a dog. But," Kylie said before pausing, "that doesn't mean I won't try."

Logan nodded, appreciative that Kylie would give it a shot, but also not wanting to get too attached to the idea.

Kylie continued, "I wish *you* could adopt her. You'd make such a good dog dad, Logan."

Logan's face started to turn red upon hearing Kylie say the term "dog dad."

"I would adopt her in a heartbeat if I could," Logan replied in a low voice.

But even if he could, Logan couldn't imagine bringing a dog, especially one as loving and happy as Clover, into his energy-depleting trailer. Clover deserved a home that radiated with love. And that's how Logan pictured Kylie and her family.

"I see," said Kylie. "Well, maybe Clover will stick around long enough for me to convince my family that we're ready for a dog."

"So your family has never had a dog?"

"No, we had a cat once when I was really young, but right now we don't have any pets. I can't wait to finally have a dog, and I can't imagine how amazing it would be if that dog was Clover. It's almost too exciting to even think about. I really shouldn't get my hopes up."

When they arrived at the school's entrance, Logan opened the door for Kylie who graciously entered following his prompt. He gave himself an internal high five for not being awkward. Things had been going smoother since he'd eliminated "waving" from his available gesture options with Kylie.

"So, I guess I'll see you in math class?" Kylie asked in an upbeat tone.

"For sure. See you then," Logan replied with his arms down by his sides.

CLOVER

The morning brought kibble that almost seemed tasteless at this point, a quick walk, and typical dog room sounds. It was a quiet day. Nothing had happened to distinguish this day from the others. I hoped that would change soon. I was ready to get out and explore again. Maybe I could go back to the trash container where Logan had found me and hang out with him today. While I'd grown more used to life in the closet, I didn't want to stay in it forever. It was just about time for me to move on.

Toward the end of the day, but before dinner time, which despite my love for food, had become less and less exciting with each passing day, Miranda entered the room with a familiar scent. The scent of the outdoors mixed with dessert. Was Logan's girl with her?

She was! She came over to my closet door with Miranda. Her excited energy was contagious. My tail wagged as I whimpered for some love.

"Hey, Clover, I see you remember Logan's friend, Kylie."

Logan? Was Logan coming, too? I couldn't smell him. And Kylie… I remembered that word when I had seen her last. Was that the girl's name? I decided to go with it. I'm ready for an adventure, Kylie! I hoped she was going to take me to the place that made her smell like cookies.

"Hi, sweet Clover."

Her voice was soft and full of warmth. She reached her hand in to pet me.

"You're even cuter than I remember, Clover," said Kylie.

Miranda turned to Kylie. "I know you mentioned that you don't have much time today, and since the weather isn't participating, feel free to just hang out in here. The dogs would love to get some one-on-one time with someone. It's really important for their wellbeing while they're here."

"Oh, I would love that. I'm assuming it won't be a problem if I start here?"

"Of course not," replied Miranda. "While I do think Clover is adjusting, she's a very independent dog. I think she's been getting a little antsy."

"I see," Kylie said as she opened my door and sat next to me on the floor. Miranda remained standing outside my closet door.

I rubbed up against Kylie's face and was thrilled when she laughed. Not everyone liked it when I did that, but it was a favorite move of mine.

"I'm sorry we can't go outside, girl. I'd love to take you on a stroll or play fetch with you, but there's just too much rain."

Rain. I barked. How did she know my old name?

"Ha, you must've gotten her excited when you said 'fetch,'" Miranda said. "I'm sure she'll play fetch with you another day, Clover."

Clover. I tilted my head as Miranda walked away. Could I have two names?

"It's just going to be you and me hanging out inside today, girl."

Kylie sat next to me in my closet for a long time. I enjoyed snuggling up to her and listening to her talk to me. She started to remind me of Gloria with everything she had to say to me. I listened intently.

"So, Clover, what do you think? Do you think I have a shot at being the lead in the choir recital next month? There are so many good singers. I'm not sure I really stand a chance."

Kylie continued on. While she was still sweet, warm, and caring, I did notice that her smile wasn't quite as prominent as it had been when Logan had been around before. I understood. Logan made me smile, too. Would Kylie be taking me in her car to go see him? What would her car smell like? I stood up with anticipation.

"Well, Clover, it's probably time for me to move on to some of the other dogs here and spend some time with them. I wish I could take you home, girl."

Home. Rain. How did she know these things? I didn't want to go home, and I was pretty sure I didn't want to be Rain again. Being Clover still needed some work since I was missing the constant love and freedom I was looking for, but surely, I could find it.

Kylie exited my closet and spent some time with each of the other dogs before she left. I could hear her giggle every now and then, but she wasn't as talkative with the other dogs as she had been with me.

When she came back to my door, she told me, "I was thinking some more, girl, and I'm going to go for it. I'm going to audition." She seemed happy and full of conviction. I hoped it meant she was about to take me out. I sat down and looked up at her with a smile. "Thanks for the talk, Clover. I'll see you this weekend for the fair with Logan."

Kylie left the room. I hoped she would come back with Logan, but I gave up on that thought when the lights finally went out and it was time for bed.

I lounged on my cot and thought about my next move. I needed to get back to the trash container. I wasn't made to live in this closet.

LOGAN

Logan grabbed his things and thought about being at the fair with Kylie and Clover. He'd played out so many scenes in his head of this day already: him and Kylie eating cotton candy while laughing at people's expressions on the tilt-a-whirl ride, winning Kylie a stuffed animal from the water gun game, walking around the fairgrounds with Clover and wondering if people thought they were boyfriend and girlfriend. More daunting thoughts had crept into Logan's mind as well. What if Kylie decided she didn't want to hang out with him at the fair? What if he couldn't win her a prize? What if…

Logan's phone rang. He didn't recognize the number, but with the day's upcoming events, he decided to answer.

"Logan?" a panicked voice asked before he had a chance to even say hello.

"Yes?"

"Logan, this is Miranda. Clover's gone. She was out for her morning walk and slipped out of a volunteer's hands and ran off."

"Oh, no…" Logan said.

"I know. I can't even believe it. But honestly, if I've learned anything from my years working with dogs, if I had to guess, she's probably trying to find you."

"How would she even know how to find me?"

"Well, dogs are pretty magnificent creatures. Their sense of smell is thousands of times stronger than ours, and their determination should never be doubted. I would suggest you wait at home to see if she turns up there."

"Well, she's never been to my home… I wonder… do you think she'd try going back to McCorley's where I found her?"

"Maybe. That's a good thought. I could try calling them. Actually, they wouldn't be open yet."

"I'll go there and check now. I'll keep you posted."

"Thanks, Logan. I truly think you'll be our best bet at finding her."

Logan hung up with Miranda and called Drew.

"Hey, are you busy?"

"Um, well, let's see… it's, uh… 8:30 on a Saturday? I can't exactly say I'm 'busy' quite yet. I'm barely awake, man. What's up?"

"Right, yeah. It's still early. Well, remember that dog I took to the rescue? Clover? She ran away this morning… and I need your help."

"Oh man, really? Once a stray, always a stray, I guess. What do you need?"

"Well, I was hoping you could come to my place, actually. Miranda, she's the rescue owner, she seems to think that Clover might end up at my place. I think if she's really trying to find me then she might be going back to where I first found her, so I'm going to start there. But in case Miranda is right, I would like someone to be here in case she shows. My dad isn't going to be home until late, so you'll have the place to yourself."

"Okay, so just like, hang at your place in hopes that a dog will show? Sounds easy enough."

"Okay, great. Can you be here in ten?"

"Yes, I'll be over soon."

Logan texted Kylie to give her the latest update on Clover. They were originally going to meet at the rescue at 9:00, so he wanted to make sure he caught her before she left. After Logan told her his plan of checking for Clover at the pub, she offered to meet him there.

CLOVER

Zoe had taken me out on a morning walk outside the fenced-in area and I knew it was going to be my best chance at a successful escape. And it was the right day. I could feel it. I knew I could find Logan.

As soon as we had stepped outside, the warmth from the sun's rays hit my fur as my paws hit the cold, damp leaves on the ground. The opposing sensations ensured that I was fully awake and ready for my latest adventure. Zoe had taken me and another smaller dog out. I felt bad knowing I was going to leave them. I didn't want Zoe to think I was running from her, but I had important things to do. I had a boy to get to, chicken to smell, and a full day outside to enjoy.

We were only a few steps in on the trail when I decided to bolt. I had given her no expectation for such behavior. I knew she wouldn't be ready for it. And just like that, I was off, out of her grasp and on my own. I'm sure Zoe must've yelled for me, and the little dog probably barked and maybe even wanted to follow, but I was focused on my getaway. The wind was whipping by my ears again, seemingly stroking my fur, and while it was technically pushing against me, it was somehow driving me forward.

I ran across the street, into the woods, and continued on through the trees, not too far from the road. I remembered the way that Logan had driven before and knew I was going in the right direction.

Even with a clear destination in mind, I still had to make a pit stop. It was early and I hadn't had my bland breakfast yet. I stopped and sniffed around in the woods but didn't find anything all too appetizing. There were some metal buckets stuck to some of the trees, but they weren't filled with anything that particularly interested me. I really shouldn't have been so picky, but after eating what I had been, I felt I deserved a hearty first meal as a free dog once again.

Then I spotted my favorite shape dotting the side of the road at the end of each house's driveway. Trash containers. YES.

I didn't hesitate. I'd never encountered a trash container I hadn't liked.

I knocked the first one down with ease and joy. Everything inside was encased neatly in bags. Luckily, I was able to break through the bags in a matter of seconds. The scents that filled the air around me were abundantly sweet and equally acidic. I downed scraps filled with familiar flavors and pieces of food that were new to my taste buds. I enjoyed every second, but also knew what would happen if I continued to eat too much. Two more bites and I was out of there. I had somewhere to get to.

I charged back across the street and into the woods as I continued to follow the road while remaining out of sight. I slowed my pace as I felt my stomach grow full but was able to carry on.

Then the woods came to an end. The road continued, but I'd be exposed. It was a good sign, though. This looked similar to the place where I'd met Logan for the first time. I hoped he would have water again when I found him. I was getting thirsty.

"Clover!"

I knew that voice.

"Clover!"

The voice was a bit louder this time.

I stopped.

"Clover!" the voice repeated, even louder.

It was Kylie. She was calling me from a car. I watched her pull over to the side of the road across the street from me. I sat down. I hadn't quite reached my destination, but I was willing to stop to say hi to Kylie.

She exited her car and ran to meet me where I waited for her across the street.

"Oh my gosh, Clover. You had us so worried! I'm so glad you're here. And safe. What were you doing, girl?"

She seemed happy to see me. And honestly, I was pretty happy to see her, too. Maybe she'd come with me to see Logan!

Kylie picked up her phone as she started to guide me toward her car by the scruff of my neck. A car ride could impede my progress, but at the same time, I wasn't able to turn down the opportunity to find out what Kylie's car was like. I hopped in her backseat and stretched out. The windows were cracked open, so there was still a slight breeze. I hadn't realized how tired I'd become since my escape. It was nice to lie down on something soft.

I could hear Kylie talk into her phone as she stood outside.

"Logan, it's Kylie. Hey, I found her. I have Clover in my backseat right now."

I heard a deep breath come out of Kylie's phone as she held it in her palm.

"Oh, thank goodness. Wow. Where did you find her?"

I heard Logan's voice coming from the phone now. He sounded panicked. What was he doing?

"I saw her running on the sidewalk and pulled over by the post office. We're only a couple of blocks from McCor- ley's, so I think you must've been right. I think she was headed back to where she met you."

Another deep breath from Logan.

"I'm so glad you found her. I'll be right there."

It turned out Kylie's car wasn't quite as thrilling as I'd hoped it would be. There wasn't anything to eat. There weren't even any old food wrappers. It was probably the cleanest car

I'd ever been in. It was filled with Kylie's curious scent, though, so that much I appreciated.

"What were you doing, girl? Huh?" Kylie asked me as she sat with me in the back. "I wish you'd known that Logan and I were already coming to get you for a fun time at the fair today."

She seemed a little upset as she spoke, but her touch was gentle, so I figured I hadn't done anything wrong.

"I'm sure you were just looking to mix up your day a little, huh? I can imagine it would get pretty lonely there at the rescue."

I wondered if Kylie thought I truly understood everything she told me.

"Here's Logan, girl. Stay. I'll be right back."

"Logan, hi."

I watched as Kylie went over to Logan and gave him a hug. I hadn't seen this action from them before, but it seemed natural.

"I'm so, so relieved you found her."

I could see Logan showing Kylie a rope that he held in his hands.

"I brought this," Logan said. "I figured we could use it as a makeshift leash. It was the best I could find at my place before I left."

"Yeah, this is great. Good idea," Kylie replied.

I barked. Why were they ignoring me? I hadn't left to find them just to be left in the back of a clean car.

Logan opened the door and slid into the backseat. I plopped on top of him. *Logan! Hi. My plan worked. I left to come see you and now you're here! Today is going to be so much fun. Maybe we can hang out all the time, and I can sleep where you sleep tonight?*

"Clover, hi. I'm so glad Kylie found you. You can't just go running away like that, though, okay? The rescue is there to keep you safe before you find your new home."

Home. There was that word again. I wondered where we'd be going next.

LOGAN

"If you'd only known that we had a big day planned for you today," Logan said to Clover as he scratched behind her ears.

Kylie sat on the other side of Clover in the backseat. Clover leaned one way then the other to ensure she was making the most of their close proximity.

"I'll let everyone know we found her," Logan said as Clover flipped over onto her back and laid her head in Kylie's lap.

Logan exited the car to call Drew.

"Hey, man."

"Hey, how's it going? Any luck?" Drew asked.

"Yeah, we found her. She wasn't far from the pub."

"Oh good, man, that's good." Drew paused. "Who's the 'we'?"

"Oh, I'm with Kylie. She's actually the one who found her."

"Ah, okay. I see now. I had to stay here so you could go out on a date, huh?"

"Uh…"

"I'm just playing. I'm glad you found your dog."

"Thanks. I mean, obviously I would've asked you to come out and help on the road, but I wasn't sure where Clover would be, and you're one of the few people that have been over to my place and…"

"No, really, I get it. I was just giving you a hard time. I'll head out now. Also, I may or may not have finished the box of cookies that was on the counter."

The cookies weren't Logan's. They were his dad's. While it was likely that his dad wouldn't even notice they were missing, there was also a chance that it could turn into an unnecessary problem for Logan. He made a mental note to pick up some more cookies on his way home later.

Drew continued, "But I guess I'll let you two lovebirds get on with your day. Peace out."

Drew hung up before Logan could respond. Logan was surprised to hear Drew's reaction to Logan being with Kylie when he'd been the one to push Logan to really go for it in the first place. It seemed like a "congrats" was more in order, really. But maybe Drew had other stuff on his mind. Logan decided to let it go.

"That was a quick call," Kylie said as Logan got back into the car.

"Yeah, it was. It was just to Drew. I'd asked him to stay on watch at my place in case Clover found her way there."

"Oh, that was a good idea," responded Kylie.

"I'll call Miranda now."

Logan informed Miranda that he and Kylie had Clover. It was almost time for the fair to start, and since Miranda said she had everything they'd need, she suggested that they come right over to the fair.

"Do you want me to drive us?" Kylie asked. "Clover seems pretty comfy, and I'm sure your car will be safe in the post office parking lot for the day."

"Um, sure."

His palms instantly became balmy.

"That sounds good," he said.

Get. It. Together.

"I'm just going to grab some things out of my car real quick," he continued. "Do you want some water?"

"Sure, thank you."

Logan saw Clover's ears perk when he said the word "water."

"Okay, I'll grab some for all of us. Be right back."

Logan had a cooler of cold water in his backseat. He was more eager to get it for his sweaty hands than his own thirst at this point.

CLOVER

I knew my plan would work, but I'd underestimated just how successful it could be. First Kylie, then Logan, and then a car ride with them both. I could fully relax in the backseat knowing that they weren't going anywhere as long as the vehicle was in motion. I'd warmed up to the clean backseat since Kylie had started driving. It provided plenty of room to stretch out without any barriers. It was unusual to me, but increasingly enjoyable. It certainly beat the closet that I'd been staying in. I was excited to never have to go back.

When the car stopped, the air was filled with sweet and smoky scents, some of which I'd never smelled before. It almost looked like a farm, but with a lot of different structures and buildings. And a lot of happy visitors.

Logan turned back to me as Kylie turned the car off. He looked like he was getting uncomfortably warm, which was odd since I found it to be quite cool and comfortable in the car. I must've had the best seat.

"So, Clover," Logan said, "we have to set a few ground rules before you leave this car. Number one: there will not be any trying to escape. No taking off. No pulling on your leash. Not even any *thinking* about running away."

I tilted my head. He seemed quite serious. Was it because he was overheating? There wasn't much I could do to help. I whimpered.

Just like that, Kylie cracked the windows. I may not always understand everything she told me, but I felt like our communication was improving.

"Number two: enough of this strict talk. Let's go have some fun!"

I could feel Logan's temperament change as his excitement flowed through the car. This was more like it! Kylie smiled and I watched both of their faces turn a darker shade as they exchanged glances.

"All right, let's go!" Kylie said.

Now those words I understood. It was time to get going. Logan retrieved me from the backseat. I still had a full stomach from my morning escapade, but the scents that swirled in the air made me wish I was hungry. I could smell meat and dessert, but in new and intriguing ways. I had to do a thorough investigation of this busy farm of structures with so many visitors. Kylie was right. *Let's go!*

LOGAN

"I think Miranda said they'd be next to the 4-H building," Logan said as the trio walked into the fair.

The day was turning out to be beautiful. The morning fog that covered the mountains and streets earlier had faded as the fall sun continued to rise.

They found Miranda and some other volunteers under a pop-up tent. Miranda had Kiwi with her on a leash. Kiwi wore a lime green vest that adorned the rescue's name. The bright color of the vest was extra eye catching against her dark fur.

"Clover!" Miranda called out upon seeing Logan and Kylie approaching with the previously lost pup.

Clover rubbed up against Miranda and sat down as if she'd never done a thing wrong.

"I'm so glad you're here," she said. "You had us worried, girl."

Zoe walked over to the group upon hearing the excitement from Miranda.

"Logan, hi," Zoe said as she rested her hand on Logan's shoulder. "I can't believe you found her! That's just amazing."

"I know!" Logan said. "And it was actually Kylie here who found her," he corrected.

"Ah, well, nice work," replied Zoe as she glanced at Kylie. "I'm glad she's safe."

"Me, too. I think she just needed some adventure," said Kylie.

"Well, she'll have plenty here today," Miranda chimed in. "Our dogs always love this place. The animals, the scents, the people. Dogs typically aren't allowed, of course, but we're allowed to be here to help promote the rescue and, hopefully, get some dogs the attention they need and deserve in order to get them adopted!"

"Yes, we can't wait to help," Logan said as he questioned himself for saying "we." Was he talking for both him *and* Kylie, now? His thoughts started to spiral.

"Hey, Logan," Kylie said to him quietly. "Are you okay? You look a little… pale."

"Sorry, yes, I'm fine. Just hungry, I guess," Logan lied. He couldn't think of a better explanation.

"Hey, Miranda, I think we're going to go grab a bite to eat if that's okay," said Kylie.

"Oh, yes, of course," replied Miranda. "While I'm excited that you're here as ambassadors for the rescue, I also want to make sure you both still enjoy yourselves today. Here, before you two take off, take this vest for Clover. If you get any questions from people that you're unable to answer, feel free to give them my card or send them my way. I'm sure you'll both do great."

"Thanks, Miranda," said Logan. "We'll check in with you later."

"All right. You two go have fun!" replied Miranda.

"Okay," Kylie said as they started to walk away from the tent, "what are you craving this morning? Fried dough? A turkey leg?" Kylie laughed as she looked around the fairgrounds. "Kind of slim pickings if you were looking for anything healthy, I guess."

"Anything will do. Is there something you're interested in?" Logan asked.

"I'm a sucker for soup in a bread bowl, actually. And fried candy bars… but maybe we save those for later in the day."

Logan pulled out his phone from his back pocket to check the time. It was 10:14. "Soup for breakfast it is!"

Logan took a deep breath. The conversation seemed much easier with Kylie now after his slip-up at the rescue tent. They walked through the crowds toward a bread bowl stand. A couple in front of them held hands as they walked slowly. Logan thought about how nice it'd be to be that couple and hold hands with Kylie at the fair. It surely wouldn't be today, he figured, with the slow rate things were progressing, but he hoped it would be someday.

CLOVER

The scents continued to astound me at the odd farm. Logan and Kylie had taken me by plenty of animals, some of which I'd seen and smelled before, and some that were completely new to me. But it was the scent of all of the food that had me most intrigued.

I sat in the grass while I watched Logan and Kylie somehow spoon out liquid from bread. I'd never witnessed any bread like this before. It seemed like they were enjoying it, but I decided to wait to bug them for a bite of food later.

They seemed like they were the only two in the world as they talked and laughed over their mysterious meal. I hoped we wouldn't stay still for too long. There was so much to see. But I was glad they were happy and together. I wondered what they would have been doing if I hadn't escaped the place with the dog room.

We stood, and I tried to ignore the feel of the cloth they'd wrapped around me earlier. Miranda had given it to Logan and Kylie. Was it a punishment for running off? I didn't mean to run away from Miranda. I just had to get out. I hoped the cloth would come off soon.

"Hey," a new voice called out as Logan and Kylie threw their trash away. "That's such a cute dog," the man said as he approached us with a young girl.

The little girl reminded me of Gloria with her long wavy hair, but she looked down and stood behind the man as she held his hand.

"Oh, thank you. This is Clover," said Logan.

I wagged my tail. I loved when Logan said my name.

"You can pet her if you'd like," Logan continued. "She's super friendly." Logan tussled the top of my head.

"Okay, thanks," the man replied. He looked to the little girl and bent down.

"Hannah, do you want to pet the dog?"

The girl twisted her body toward the man and smiled.

I stayed still.

Logan reached his hand down to pet me again, and Kylie bent down and faced the young girl.

"I promise she's friendly. And she *loves* when someone pets her," encouraged Kylie to the girl.

Kylie was petting me now, too, as the two strangers continued to look on.

"Do you both work at the rescue?" asked the man. "I see she's a rescue dog?"

"We just started volunteering there," said Kylie. "It's such a wonderful place. And Clover here is a very special dog."

"I see," said the man. "See, Hannah? She's a sweet dog."

The girl continued to smile as she twirled slightly from side to side, remaining close to the man as he reached out to pet me. The girl was apprehensive about something. I knew it was best if I remained where I was.

"Well," the man continued, "I guess we're not quite ready for a dog, but we'll work on it. I appreciate the opportunity to meet Clover. Thank you, both. Enjoy the fair!"

"Thank you. You, too!" replied Kylie before turning to Logan. "Well, this seems easy enough, huh?"

Logan looked down at his feet. "Yes, I guess it does."

He didn't seem as excited as he'd been before the man and girl had come over.

"Is everything okay?" asked Kylie.

"Yeah, sorry. That just got me thinking that people might really be interested in adopting Clover."

"I know, that's a great thing." Kylie said before she paused. "Isn't it?"

"It is. She's amazing. She deserves a great home."

Logan kicked some dirt as he continued to stare down.

"I just..." he continued. "It's hard to imagine not having her around, you know? That probably sounds crazy since I haven't known her that long. But I feel connected to her. At the same time," Logan said as he looked up at Kylie, "I know I won't be able to keep her. So then I start to wonder about whether you'd be able to take her again. I just want to make sure she ends up with someone she loves and trusts. She deserves that."

"Aw, it's almost heartbreaking how much you love Clover," Kylie replied.

I looked up at the sound of my name. Was it time for the next odd-farm event?

"I love Clover," Kylie said. "And I would love to adopt her. I just think it might take some major convincing for my family to say yes, but I'm still planning on trying."

Logan stood a little straighter.

"I can help," Logan said picking up his pace. "If your family needs a reference, I can write something, or they can call me, or maybe Miranda can speak to them. I'm sure she'd be willing to help…"

"Okay, okay, slow down. It will be okay. No matter what, Clover is, and will be, loved. Just look at her," said Kylie. "She's going to be okay."

The pair gazed at me as I looked back and forth at them with a smile as I panted. There seemed to be a lot of talking about me but not a lot of doing anything with me. I was ready to get a move on.

"And in the meantime," said Kylie, "I'll see what I can do. My family is actually planning on coming to the fair today."

LOGAN

Logan wished he still had his chilled water bottle to clutch as his palms began to sweat again. He didn't feel ready to meet Kylie's family. The day had already provided enough emotions for him. How would he be able to handle meeting the family of his first serious crush today too?

Then, the two small Clovers appeared on Logan's shoulders again.

I can confirm you're not ready for this, said the Clover on the left as she yawned. *There's no way.*

Logan, you'll be fine. It's not a big deal. Just breathe, said the good Clover.

Heh, yeah, get your breathing in now because you won't be able to later, replied the other Clover.

Look at it this way, said the good Clover. *This is an opportunity to help me find the right home. You could help convince her family that I'm the right dog for them.*

That's just what Logan needed to hear and focus on. He wouldn't let meeting Kylie's family mess with his head. He would stay focused on making sure they knew how great Clover was.

"Logan?" Kylie asked as she looked over to him with a furrowed brow. "Are you sure you're good? Did the food not help?"

"Sorry, yes, I'm fine," replied Logan. "That's great that your family is coming to the fair today. I'm sure they'll love Clover, too."

"Yes, for sure," replied Kylie. "At least my mom and little sister will. That much is just about guaranteed. It's my dad who will most likely be less interested. He still doesn't think we can handle taking care of a dog."

"I think you'd be an amazing dog mom," said Logan before he could second guess his word choice.

"Thanks, Logan. That's really sweet."

The pair's hands grazed each other as they walked, causing Logan to experience what felt like electricity spark and ignite throughout his body. Both Kylie and Logan knew how special Clover was, but Logan was starting to realize more and more just how special Kylie was to him.

"Hey," said Kylie as she tapped Logan's arm with the back of her hand. "There's my mom and sister right there over by the horse-pulling arena."

Kylie picked up her pace as Logan tried to keep up. Clover seemed more excited now that it appeared that the couple had a clearer destination in mind. Logan tried not to think about what was going to happen next. He took a few deep breaths as he followed Kylie toward the arena.

"Mom! Vicky! Hey!" Kylie called out.

The family hugged as they greeted each other. Logan smiled at the outpouring of affection that he was witnessing.

"Mom, Vicky, this is my friend, Logan. He's also volunteering at the rescue. Logan, this is my mom, Andrea, and my little sister, Vicky."

Logan shook hands with Andrea and Vicky as Clover nudged his other hand with her nose.

"Hi, Logan," said Andrea. "It's very nice to meet you. I'm so glad to hear that Kylie has a friend to volunteer with. That's very impressive for you both to take the time to help the animals at the rescue."

"Thanks, Andrea. It's nice to meet you, too."

So far, so good, Logan thought.

Clover nudged Logan's hand again.

"It looks like someone else is waiting to get introduced," Kylie said as she giggled. "This," she said with her arms extended for the grand introduction, "is Clover. She's a Nova Scotia Duck Tolling Retriever."

"Oh my, she's beautiful," said Andrea as she and Vicky went to pet Clover.

"She's so cute!" Vicky said. She bent down and Clover took the opportunity to lick her cheek.

"Logan, here, is actually the one who found her on the street and brought her to the rescue," Kylie said.

"Ah, even more impressive," said Andrea.

Logan blushed. While he appreciated the compliments, he was ready for this unplanned encounter to be over.

"She's a really exceptional dog, as you can tell," Logan said.

Clover gave Vicky another lick on the cheek.

"And it looks like she really likes you, Vicky," Logan said.

Everyone laughed as Clover continued to cuddle up to Kylie's sister. Logan smiled and his shoulders started to relax.

"Mom, you'll have to stop by the rescue tent later and meet the rescue owners, Miranda and Ben."

"Oh, sure. We'll come by later after we have some lunch," said Andrea.

"Great," Kylie replied. "And is Dad coming?"

"He may stop by later. He had to deal with a work thing this morning," said Andrea.

"Okay, well the rescue tent is right next to the 4-H barn. Text me when you head over later."

"Will do," said Andrea. "You two have fun!"

CLOVER

The scent of the people we walked away from reminded me of Kylie and another familiar scent that I couldn't fully place. I liked these people. They were loving and generous with their attention. I was excited to see who we'd meet next.

Shortly after we left the new people, Kylie began walking me. It was weird to not have Logan in charge of me, but I enjoyed having Kylie take over. With every change in direction, she would say things like, "we're going to go this way, Clover," and, "time to go left now, girl." I was never forgotten.

When we stopped at one of the many booths with people inside, I knew things were going to get exciting.

"Can we each get a set of five darts, please?" Logan asked the man inside the booth as he handed him a piece of paper.

The man placed a few items in front of Logan and Kylie and unenthusiastically said, "Three popped balloons, and you win."

"Think I can win one of the elephants up there?" Logan asked Kylie as he pointed to the large stuffed animals that lined the top of the booth.

I never understood what excited people about stuffed animals when there were real animals around. They knew I was still here, right? I tugged at the leash.

"Well, I think Clover here is trying to say yes," Kylie said while laughing and looking down at me. "Do you think he can win the biggest prize, girl? Or do you think *I* will? I think that might be more likely. What do you think, Clover?" Kylie asked as she continued to chuckle.

I wish I could understand her. She seemed so happy with her question. They both looked down at me. I tugged again.

"I see," said Logan. "One vote for me, one vote for Kylie? That's fair, that's fair. I understand that you don't want to show your favoritism in front of her when we're trying to get her family to adopt you. It makes sense, it does," Logan said to me with a smile before glancing over at Kylie.

"Oh, wow," Kylie said. "I see you have a competitive streak, huh?"

"It does appear to be that way," replied Logan as he shot his arm back and forth before releasing one of the items on the table.

It reminded me of his arm motions when he'd seen Miranda at the place with the dog room. Was something still wrong with his car? I was glad we had taken Kylie's.

Then, to my surprise, Kylie made a similar motion. But her movement was followed by a sudden popping noise that caused me to bark. Where had that come from? Kylie and Logan didn't seem rattled, though. Kylie started laughing as Logan threw another one of the objects, but no popping sound followed. Kylie's motions continued to be followed by loud noises while Logan's arm actions were followed by silence. After a couple more popping sounds, Kylie jumped up and down joyfully.

The man in the booth handed Kylie one of the large stuffed animals from the top of the booth. Logan watched with a grin.

I sat down and whimpered. Did she need that if I was right here? Could I chew it?

Kylie giggled and petted me.

"Everything's okay, Clover," she said. "My giant elephant prize isn't going to hurt you."

I lunged at it.

"But you can't bite it, either," said Kylie in a more authoritative tone.

I decided to ignore the oversized stuffed animal in hopes they would, too.

LOGAN

"I still can't believe you won that."

"Oh, tell me you're not one of those guys that thinks they have to win the prize for the girl."

"No, no, I'm not saying that, necessarily. I mean, I would've *liked* to have won you the prize, but I just can't believe that each of your darts hit a balloon every single time!"

"It probably *would* be hard to believe when you're someone that didn't even hit one."

"Oh, ouch. Who's the competitive one now?"

"I do have a competitive side. I'll admit that," Kylie said with a smirk.

Logan smiled as he realized how easily things were flowing between them.

"Do you want me to carry your insanely large elephant prize for you?"

"Oh, are you making fun of it now? This prize took skill! I can carry it for now, thank you. I was actually thinking we could drop it off at the rescue tent. I'm hoping my family will be going over there soon. I'll text my sister and let her know we're headed over."

So much for the easy flow that had taken over Logan's time with Kylie. He felt a knot twist in his stomach as he realized he might have to meet Kylie's dad soon.

"Good idea," Logan replied. "But at least let me take Clover for now, then."

Kylie handed him the leash. He was relieved to have something to distract him from the dread of meeting Kylie's father.

"Hey," Logan said as they neared the tent, "isn't that your family at the tent talking to Miranda?"

"Huh, yeah, I think so. I guess they beat us there."

"Kylie, hey," Andrea called out upon seeing her daughter approach the tent. "Miranda, here, was just telling us about Clover's escape operation this morning! You didn't tell me that! I'm so glad you found her."

"Us, too!" Kylie replied.

"We are as well," Miranda chimed in. "These two have already proved themselves to be wonderfully reliable and caring volunteers. We're lucky to have them."

"That's so nice to hear," Andrea replied.

"I was also telling your family about our foster program. Since Clover clearly enjoys some more freedom, I think she'd be a great candidate for the program, and if your family is interested, I could set them up with an application right here today. Then I'd just need a few pictures of your home's yard, and if all goes well, you could take Clover home by the end of the weekend."

Logan was elated by what he was hearing. This was everything he wanted for Clover.

"Oh my gosh, Mom, are you really considering this? That would be amazing. I know I haven't volunteered for long, but Clover is so wonderful. And you and Dad and Vicky could get to know her better if we were fostering her, and I can show you how great it would be."

Andrea smiled and nodded her head as Kylie spoke.

"I agree, honey," Andrea replied. "And seeing you walk around here with Clover today does make me want a dog even more. Plus, I have to say, I'm intrigued by the fostering idea. I like that we wouldn't necessarily have to commit to making such a major change in the household without testing it out first," Andrea replied as something caught her eye behind Kylie. "But… I think the one you really need to convince is behind you."

CLOVER

I recognized the scent of the newcomer before I even turned to see him. Peppermint and leather. It was the standoffish man who Miranda had shown around the rescue the other day. I sensed a change in the group's energy with his presence. I wasn't thrilled to see him again.

"Hey, what's everyone up to over here?" the man asked.

"Roy, hey," said the woman, "come meet Miranda, the owner of Kiwi Canine Rescue where Kylie is volunteering. She was just telling us about this sweet dog here, Clover."

"Yes, very cute dog," the man replied without acknowledging me as he approached Miranda. "Miranda, hi. Nice to meet you."

"Ah, yes," said Miranda slowly, "hi. Nice to meet you, too." She half smiled as she squinted her eyes and shook his hand.

I knew Miranda knew this man, but she didn't greet him like an old friend. I didn't, either.

"I was just telling your family here about our fostering opportunities. I was pleased to hear that you all might be interested," Miranda said to the man.

"Oh, well, I don't know about that. Kylie is attempting to prove herself as a responsible potential dog owner, but she just started volunteering. I don't think we're ready for a dog at this point," replied the man.

"Oh, come on, Dad," said the younger girl.

"Yeah, come on," Kylie and the woman added in unison.

"I will say," said Miranda, "that Clover here is the perfect candidate for our foster program. She's well acclimated to being around people. In fact, she seems to even prefer people over dogs. She's also taken quite a liking to your daughter and her friend Logan, here."

"I see," said the man. "I'm glad you're making friends with the dogs, Kylie."

Kylie rolled her eyes and then offered a slight smile to Logan.

"Dad, I want you to meet Logan," said Kylie. "Logan Greenfield. Logan, this is my dad, Roy."

"Ah, yes, Greenfield. You must be Dave's boy?"

"Yes, sir," replied Logan sounding confident, but his shoulders slumped.

I nudged his hand. I wanted him to stand up to this non-dog-lover.

"It's nice to meet you," Logan said.

"Yes, you, too. Well, I've got to get back to work, but I'm glad I stopped by to see what you all were up to. I have to admit, I didn't quite expect this."

"So we can foster her, right?" the younger girl asked hopefully.

"I'll leave that up to your mom. I've got to run."

The man left without petting me once. I huffed but was pleased when both Logan and Kylie reached for my head to pet me at the same time.

Excitement rose in the group again as Miranda talked about paperwork and opportunities.

Kylie and Logan smiled at each other.

"I can't believe this is really going to work out," Kylie said.

"I can," Logan replied. "I really couldn't picture anything else." He looked down at his feet. "Do you think your dad will warm up to Clover, though?"

"I know he doesn't seem all that into dogs, but he'll come around," said Kylie. "He likes to appear macho in front of new people. Clover will be his pal in no time."

"Okay, well that's great then," Logan said as he bent down to face me. "Clover, I know you don't know what's going on yet, but we're trying to get you a home. You're going to live with Kylie soon."

I could tell what Logan was saying was important. I sat and looked into his eyes patiently. Were we about to go somewhere else? I was ready to follow him and Kylie to the next destination, especially if it involved dinner.

LOGAN

"So, what will happen next?" Logan asked Miranda after Kylie's family had left.

"Well, we'll have to keep Clover at the rescue tonight while we process all of the paperwork. If everything looks good, which I'm sure it will, Clover will be going home with you tomorrow, Kylie."

"Oh my gosh," said Kylie. "I seriously can't believe this is happening. I have to be the luckiest person in the world right now."

"Clover, here, is pretty lucky herself," Miranda replied.

Logan subtly nodded in agreement.

"She's probably not going to like being back at the rescue tonight after her little stunt this morning, but I'm sure she'll manage just fine," said Miranda. "Now, you two go enjoy the rest of the day here, okay? Want to meet back here around 3:00 to help pack up?"

"Yes, sounds like a plan," said Logan.

Logan handed Clover's leash to Kylie.

"I guess you should probably take this now, huh?" Logan asked.

"Oh, no. That's okay. You can hang onto her for now. I'll be spending plenty of time with her soon enough. I still can't believe this is really going to happen!"

Kylie bent down to face Clover while Logan continued to hold her leash.

"I'm so excited, girl. You're going to come home with me tomorrow. Just one more night at the rescue. It won't be too bad. Just no running away this time, okay? Logan and I will bring you back there later this afternoon, and we'll go over the plan again. Everything will be all right."

Logan smiled as he took in Kylie's words. Even though she was talking to Clover, he appreciated her reassurance that everything was going to be okay.

"So, Kylie, since you'll be fostering Clover, do you think you'll still volunteer?"

As grateful as Logan was for Clover to be getting the best home possible, it was starting to dawn on him that the reason Kylie was even volunteering at the rescue to begin with was about to be achieved.

"Oh, I'll still be volunteering," said Kylie. "I know my original intention was to prove myself to my family, but I love everything about volunteering at the rescue. Including the time I get to spend with you."

Whoa. Had she really just said that? It shouldn't have been surprising, really. It seemed obvious that they both enjoyed spending time with each other, but to say it out loud like that? He hadn't expected her to be so direct.

"I…" Logan started. Was he going to share that he felt the same? It'd be safer to just change the topic. *Push forward,* he told himself. It was time to take his shot. "…enjoy spending time with you, too," he finished.

Logan and Kylie slowed their pace before coming to a stop. Clover looked back at them in time to witness their hands reach for each other's and interlock.

The moment had come. Logan was holding hands with a girl at the fair. What he'd envisioned and wanted earlier in the day had just become real, and it was happening with the only person he wanted it to happen with.

"I'm proud of you," Kylie said.

"For?"

"This."

She picked up their clasped hands.

Oh no, Logan thought, *what did she mean?* He willed himself to avoid breaking out in a panicky sweat.

"You've just been, nervous, it seems," continued Kylie, "when we're around each other."

She was still being so direct. What was happening? Logan's mind went blank.

"I guess what I'm trying to say," Kylie continued, "is that I'm happy."

Logan gulped. He didn't know how to say things the way she was saying them.

"I, uh, guess I have been pretty nervous." Logan replied. "I, um, wasn't sure if you were all that into me, I guess."

Kylie chuckled.

"Well, now you know," she said as she lightly squeezed Logan's hand.

CLOVER

I was sitting, stunned. Logan and Kylie's energy had transformed so quickly right in front of my eyes. Logan's body had relaxed while Kylie's seemed to reverberate with love and affection. I watched them as their hands remained clasped in one another's. Logan's arms and hands were always a fun source of entertainment for me.

We slowly made our way back to the spot where we'd entered the odd farm earlier in the day. Kylie and Logan sat on a wood railing. I tried not to move as the couple continued to have their special moment. It was almost like they didn't see anything else around them but each other. I knew what that was like. It was the same sensation I experienced when eating from a trash container.

The thought of food reminded me that it had been a while since my last meal. I scanned the area for scraps. There was an overflowing trash container nearby, but out of reach. Luckily, it appeared that some of its contents had blown onto the grass. I backed up ever so slightly and watched as the couple remained in their own undisturbed world, muttering things to each other that I couldn't distinguish while their hands remained intertwined.

I turned around as stealthily as possible and pawed at a paper plate, uncovering an oddly shaped piece of flat bread covered in white powder. It smelled sweet. After a quick test lick, I scarfed the mystery product down. How could scrumptious food like this end up in the trash, especially at a place with so many people? Had no one wanted these leftovers?

I was pleased with myself for not getting caught. I was starting to wonder about dinner again, though. Whatever ended up happening, I knew it would have to be better than what I'd been eating in the dog room.

I looked over at Kylie and Logan. I still didn't want to interrupt them, so I chose to lie down and close my eyes. I loved to lie in the grass and bask in the sun, and I was with two of my favorite people. There really wasn't much I would change about the day. I had to think that Logan and Kylie felt the same.

LOGAN

Logan felt like he was floating. He'd never experienced another time where he felt so light and free. There wasn't one concern on his mind as he continued to hold hands with Kylie. The connection was strong, almost electric. He would've been happy if time stopped right then and there.

"Is that Miranda walking this way?" Kylie asked, bringing Logan back to reality.

"Yes," replied Logan. "I think it must be. I guess it's time to get going."

"Yes, I guess so. I wouldn't mind staying like this, though," said Kylie.

Logan smiled since he was having the exact same thought.

"Clover, it's time to head out, girl," said Logan.

Clover's ears perked up and she sat up appearing ready to go.

"Do you think she'll be disappointed to be back at the rescue?" Kylie asked.

"I do, but it'll be worth it come tomorrow," Logan said.

"Hey, are you two ready to go?" Miranda asked as she approached the couple.

"Yeah, sorry that we didn't make it back to the tent," Logan said. "I guess we lost track of time."

"Oh, no problem. If you can just grab a few of these signs here, that would be great," Miranda said as she struggled to untangle her armful of rescue signs.

"Sure," replied Logan as he handed Clover's leash to Kylie so he could assist Miranda.

"Thank you," said Miranda. "I hope you both had a good time. It was a really great day for the rescue. I talked to a lot of people that hadn't heard of us before, so I'm glad we're getting the word out. The more people that know about us, the more dogs we'll be able to place in loving homes. And," Miranda continued, "I think the cherry on top of this day, is you, Clover." She gave Clover a big pat on her head. "Are you beyond thrilled, Kylie?"

"Yes, I think I might even be in shock! I know it's just fostering for now, but I have a good feeling about it. It's really been a great day," Kylie said as she grinned and glanced over to Logan.

"Well thank you for coming out today," Miranda said. "I'll see you both back at the rescue."

When Kylie parked her car at the rescue, Clover whimpered.

"Well, there's that disappointment we were expecting," Kylie said.

"Yes, I guess so," Logan said. He turned around to face Clover in the backseat.

"It's okay, girl. It's just one more night. We promise."

Logan felt more confident about saying the word "we" this time. Kylie had made her feelings clear, so he told himself that there wasn't a need to stress anymore. He figured he should be more focused on Clover in that moment anyway.

"Yeah, it's okay, Clover," Kylie said as she turned around to pet her. "We'll see you tomorrow, girl. Or, well, will you be able to come here tomorrow too, Logan?"

"Um, it depends. I do have to work, but just let me know when you all plan on heading over and I'll see what I can do."

"Okay, sounds good. I'll text you tomorrow."

CLOVER

I didn't understand what was happening. I wasn't supposed to be back here. I couldn't go back to the cold floor and the bland food. I had escaped! Didn't Logan and Kylie know that I'd just left this place this morning? I was supposed to be with them forever now.

I pawed at Kylie and looked over at Logan. This wasn't what I wanted. I hadn't taken off this morning just to end up back here again tonight. They had to do something.

While they spoke to me with seemingly understanding tones, they clearly didn't get what I was saying. But something about the love they showed for me made me comply as they brought me back inside.

Back in my closet, both Kylie and Logan joined me before they left. They continued to pet me and talk to me with reassuring sounds. I could hear the food being prepared. I sighed, then thought about the treats I'd had earlier in the day. I guess I could deal with another bland meal tonight. Maybe it wouldn't be forever. I had to believe they'd come back for me.

"We've got to go, girl," said Kylie as she caressed my ears.

I was starting to enjoy the way she petted me the most. She hit all the good spots.

"But I'll be back tomorrow to get you, okay?"

I nudged her arm. I didn't understand, but I wanted to. She seemed sad, but hopeful. I had similar feelings. I looked over to Logan.

"I'll see you soon too, girl. Be good."

He petted me while I breathed in his faint chicken scent. I knew I would miss both of them tonight.

I ate my dinner quickly while attempting to pretend that it was as good as other dinners I'd had before. I envisioned the contents of the trash container from earlier in the day as I drifted to sleep that night, setting myself up for some satisfying dreams.

When I awoke the next morning, I felt rested and curious. I wondered what the day would bring.

LOGAN

Logan woke seconds before his phone alarm chimed at 7:45. It was Sunday morning and the first things he thought of were Kylie and Clover. Today was the big day.

He looked at his phone. Nothing from Kylie. He had to get to work by 10:00 for a staff meeting before they opened at 11:00. The staff meetings were new, and Logan felt that they were also pointless. They were something that Bill had introduced, and all of the staff members were convinced that he just liked them as an opportunity to have people act like they were listening to him. Unless Kylie and her family were getting up super early to get Clover, his chances of being present for Clover's foster moment seemed slim.

If he didn't hear from Kylie by 8:30, he planned on texting her. If he didn't hear back by 9:00, he'd go to the rescue to wish Clover luck before he went to work.

As Logan went to the kitchen, he scanned the living room for signs of his father. He didn't see him on the couch or in his chair, so Logan figured he'd actually made it to his bedroom the night before. Then Logan noticed the countertop.

It was covered with items from the pantry. Pasta boxes, soup cans, cereal boxes. What happened there?

Logan heard a low groan from the living room.

"Who said you could eat my cookies?"

"Uh," Logan replied as he searched for where his dad was hiding.

Then he saw him on the floor in their dimly lit living room lying next to the couch.

"I didn't," Logan replied. "Drew did. I meant to pick some up yesterday, but…"

"Who's Drew?" Logan's father asked as he rolled to his side on the floor.

"My friend Drew? Short, brown hair, sings in the choir at school…"

"Eh. Anyway, need my cookies," he replied as he placed a pillow over his face to block out any light as he went back to sleep.

Logan was too focused on Clover's big day to let this irritate him. He laughed to himself as he thought about how, with his dad curled up on the floor asking for treats as soon as he woke up in the morning, it was almost like he did actually have a dog.

His dad was passed out again, but Logan knew he had to fix the cookie situation before he took off for the day. Typically, he would've remembered to pick up the cookies like he'd planned to yesterday after the fair, but the handholding and the Clover-planning hadn't allowed Logan's mind to focus on much else.

By the time Logan had replaced the cookies and was ready to officially take off for the day, it was almost 9:00. No word from Kylie. He drove to the rescue. He checked his phone upon arriving and saw he had two new messages from Kylie. His heartbeat quickened as he opened them.

I had so much fun with you yesterday. I hope to see you again today. My family will be at the rescue early this afternoon to sort out the final details with Miranda. I can't believe we'll be bringing Clover home soon!

Logan found himself smiling as he looked down at his phone. He hoped to see Kylie again today, too, even though it probably wasn't going to happen.

Logan replied: *Good morning. I had a great time with you too. I'm so glad you'll be taking Clover home today. I'll be working from 10-6, but I'll text you tonight. Enjoy your big day!*

Logan sent the message and sank back in his seat. It had begun to sprinkle outside. As Logan watched the small drops of rain cover his windshield, he wondered if he should even go into the rescue since he wouldn't be staying long.

Then he pictured Clover alone in her kennel and decided he had to see how she was doing.

Zoe greeted Logan as he entered the dog room.

"Hey, I didn't know you were volunteering today," Zoe said with a grin. "I'm so happy to see you. The more hands the better on a bad weather day like this."

"Oh, sorry I won't be able to help, Zoe. I'm just stopping in to see Clover real quick before I head to work. I'm hoping to come by after school one day this week, though."

"Ah, okay. Well, I'll look forward to that time then. Clover has already been out and had her breakfast, so she should be as joyful and excitable as ever."

"Great, thanks, Zoe. I hope today goes okay for you," Logan replied as he made his way toward Clover's kennel.

CLOVER

Logan! Hi! Please come in my closet! Are you here to take me back to the weird farm from yesterday? I'm ready to go!

Logan entered my closet, and I snuggled up to him as he sat on the cold floor. I hadn't been thrilled to be back here after my escape, but I was starting to feel better about the day ahead.

"Hey, Clover," Logan said.

I rubbed up against him more as he began talking to me. His scent was filled with chicken just the way I liked it. Was he finally going to take me to the place that made him obtain this drool-worthy smell?

"Today's a big day, Clover. Kylie and her family are going to come and get you later, okay? You're going to go home today."

Home. Today. Logan seemed happy as he was talking, but I wasn't sure if he should be.

"I'm so happy for you, girl. You deserve the absolute best."

We sat in silence for a couple minutes. I pawed at his arm when he stopped petting me.

"I've got to get going soon. I wish I could've taken you out to play, but it's a bit too muddy from the rain."

Home. Rain. Today. What was happening?

I whimpered.

"It's okay, girl. Today is a good day. I promise."

His tone continued to be reassuring, but I no longer felt positive about the day ahead.

I napped on my cot after Logan left. I didn't recall any dreams, but I started to picture my old life on the farm again when I'd been called Rain. Would I ever see that place again?

When I awoke from my next nap, I was excited to see Miranda and Kylie at my door.

"Hey, girl," Kylie said with a huge grin.

"Come on, Clover. It's an exciting day!" Miranda said as she slipped a rope around my neck and led me to a room while Kylie followed.

The woman and girl from the day before at the odd farm were in the room. The unwelcoming peppermint and leather man was there, too. The woman and the girl pleasantly greeted me. I sat down next to Kylie and stared at the man.

He stared back.

I barked.

"Looks like we're off to a good start," the man said with a huff.

He laughed a little and seemed more approachable as he did. I took a couple of steps toward him to see if he would match my advance. He extended a hand, but there wasn't anything in it. I stayed still for a moment, then took another step closer.

"There we go," said the woman. "Progress."

"It's okay, girl," Kylie said. "This is my dad."

She petted me as she spoke.

"He's just not used to dogs, but I'm sure you two will get along great eventually."

I took another step toward the man, bringing me close enough for him to pet me. He reached his hand out farther, then ruffled the top of my head. It was brief, and I could tell he wasn't used to this sort of thing. Maybe he just had to get used to me. I sat down next to him as the group chuckled and smiled.

"I think you'll all love Clover," said Miranda. "Your family is a great match for her."

LOGAN

Logan had survived the staff meeting, which had droned on for an entire forty-five minutes; worked for about half of his shift; and finally stepped outside for a break. It was a slow day at River Ridge Chicken and Logan was eager to talk to Kylie. He glanced down at his phone. It was a little after 2:30. No word from Kylie. If anything had gone awry with Clover's pickup, he assumed he would've heard, so he took this as a good sign.

"How's it going, man?" Seth said as he strolled over to Logan after getting out of his car. "Haven't seen you in a while."

"I know. Hey, thanks again for working out those schedule changes with me last time. I really appreciate it."

"Yeah, no problem. As long as you don't forget our car-wash deal. My car is looking pretty rough lately. Why'd you need that time off anyway?"

"Would you believe me if I said it was for volunteer work?"

"Ha, yeah. I would if there was some other reason associated with it. I'm thinking there's a high probability that this has to do with a chick?" Seth asked as he took out a cigarette.

He offered one to Logan who shook his head no. Logan had never accepted, but in a weird way, he appreciated how Seth continued to offer, even if it was just a smokers' habit.

"Well…"

"Yup, knew it," Seth gloated. "I absolutely knew it. So, was it worth it? At least tell me if you got her attention."

"Yeah, I, uh, believe I do," Logan said, not wanting to say too much out of respect for Kylie. "Actually, remember that stray dog that was eating out of the trash by McCorley's?"

"Yeah, I think so. Do you know what happened to it?"

"Yeah, I actually brought her to the canine rescue that day. That's where I've been volunteering. The girl I've been volunteering with is actually going to start fostering that dog today."

"Fostering, huh?" Seth asked as he blew out a puff of smoke. "I didn't even know you could do that for dogs."

"Yeah, I'm hoping it leads to her adoption, but they're going to take it slow, so we'll see."

"Well, for your sake, I hope things don't move slow for you, if you know what I mean," Seth said with a smug laugh as he dropped his cigarette and stepped on it with a quick twist of his sneaker and walked inside. Logan stayed outside for a few more minutes, leaning against the wall as he replayed his time at the fair with Kylie in his mind.

CLOVER

Kylie had repeated the word "home" to me as we drove away from Miranda's place with the dog room. I'd concluded that she must have been talking about *her* home. The home that I was now in.

It was weird to be at Kylie's house with so many people inside, all seemingly excited that I was in there with them. It smelled like her and the people I'd met at the odd farm. I wasn't sure how long I'd be here before I was taken back to the dog room, so I was ready to relish in every moment.

Kylie took me around the house and showed me the different rooms. There were stairs right when you walked in. They weren't like other stairs I had been on outside. These looked fluffy and fun. I'd have to try them out later.

To the right of the stairs, there was a room with a slippery floor, a large table, and many chairs. It didn't seem all that inviting. I was excited to go into the next room: the kitchen. I was most familiar with this type of room. The kitchen was the first room when you entered the house at the farm I used to live at. I spent the majority of my indoor time at the farm in the kitchen, mostly when the farmer wasn't home.

Kylie's kitchen was filled with alluring scents. The family laughed while I sniffed every which way as I scoped out the area.

"Maybe we should give her a treat," the young girl said.

"Good idea," said Kylie while she looked around the room.

Was she smelling all of the good scents, too? I wasn't sure what to focus on, either.

"This might do," said the woman that Kylie called Mom.

"An old apple?" asked the man who I was still unsure of. "Well that doesn't seem too appealing, does it? I think we might have some bacon left in the fridge."

"Oh wow," said Kylie, "you're warming up to Clover faster than I expected."

"Well, if I were a dog that'd been stuck in a cage, I think I'd be ready for a nice hearty piece of bacon at this point, right?"

"I completely agree. I'm sure she'll appreciate it. And I'm happy to see you're thinking of her so much," said Mom.

"I know Clover's a girl, but she's the closest thing I have to another guy around here," said the man.

He extended his hand and displayed a delectable piece of meat. I was hesitant to take it at first, not completely sure if it was for me, but it smelled too good to pass up. I snatched the piece of meat quickly and softly from the man's hand. He petted me on the head. Kitchens rarely let me down. I continued to salivate as the meat taste lingered on my tongue. What else did they have to offer?

I walked over to Kylie and nudged her hand, hoping she'd feed me next, but she just laughed and led me around the corner to the next room which had large furniture for people to sit on. Kylie pointed me to an oversized cushy pillow on the floor and had me lie down on it. I rolled over so Kylie could rub my belly.

"It looks like she likes it!" said the young girl.

"I think so!" Kylie said. "Good choice, Vicky."

I realized Vicky must be the name of the young girl. She reminded me of Kylie with her long hair and gentle nature.

The rest of the house tour brought on a mix of excitement and confusion. I wasn't sure what was going on exactly, but there were plenty of new and fun things to focus on. There was a bathroom that had a basket with a heaping pile of clothes covered in strong human scents that I couldn't wait to sink my nose into. The room that smelled most like Kylie had a bed covered in pillows, and Vicky's room was filled with tempting stuffed animals. A few even looked like dog toys. I took one and gnawed at it to see if I could get it to squeak, but Kylie took it from me and told me "no." I guessed playtime would be another time.

As it started to get dark outside, I was shown where I could relieve myself in the backyard. When I came back into the house, I noticed the kitchen smelled even more appetizing than before. The family was chopping food and tending to pots and pans. I sat down next to Kylie in the kitchen and looked up at her expectantly. It had been a while since I'd had breakfast, and that little piece of meat I'd received earlier hadn't done much to curb my appetite. It didn't seem like they were taking me back to Miranda and the dog room tonight, so I was ready to see what sort of dinner they'd be whipping up for me.

I went into the room with the sitting furniture and rested on the large pillow that Kylie had shown me earlier. I decided to wait there until someone had food for me, but if it took too long, I was ready to alert Kylie. I closed my eyes and wondered how long I'd get to stay here. And when would I see Logan again?

LOGAN

After Logan's work shift ended, he got in his car and took out his phone. He smiled when he saw a message from Kylie. It was a picture of Clover lying on a dog bed at her house. Logan felt filled with gratitude after seeing Clover in Kylie's warm and loving home.

It was shortly after 6:00 and Logan wanted so badly to catch up with Kylie and see how her day had gone with Clover. He texted to see if she had time to call. No response. He realized that her family probably ate dinner together, so he may not hear from her until later. They hadn't talked on the phone before, but today was too big of a day to just text. He had to hear how things were going.

He heated up some store-brand ravioli and sat on the couch to watch TV since his dad wasn't home. He could see the cookies he'd replaced remained untouched on the counter, but he still felt it'd been worth the trip so he wouldn't have to hear about them again.

After about an hour, his phone rang.

"Logan?" Kylie asked as Logan held his phone to his ear. "Are you there?"

"Yes, um, hi," Logan replied as he muted the TV. Had he not actually said anything when he'd answered the call? He took a deep breath and cleared his throat. "How's everything going? How's Clover doing?"

"I can't believe how well things are going," Kylie said. "Clover seems right at home. We gave her a tour of the house and my dad even fed her real bacon."

Logan felt incredibly relieved and cracked a smile. "Oh man, she must've loved that. She's probably his biggest fan now."

"Yeah, I'm really in awe at how perfect today was. And she's finally here, at my house. Which will hopefully become her permanent home."

"Yeah, so how will all of that work exactly?" Logan asked as he turned off the TV and went to his room.

"Well, Miranda explained more of that today. We can foster her for up to two weeks before we'd need to make the decision to adopt her permanently. Otherwise, if someone else is interested in her after two weeks, we'd have to give her up. But if someone is interested in her *before* the two weeks are up, we can still hold on to her if we haven't decided."

"Okay. And you'd probably have your minds made up before two weeks, right?"

"Yeah, I don't see why we wouldn't."

"She must be so happy to be home with you."

"She's had dinner, so I think she's just about as happy as she can be!"

Logan laughed. "She does love her food," he replied as Kylie joined in with the laughter.

"For sure. Now she's just lying down at the foot of my bed."

"Oh, nice. She's even allowed on the furniture!" Logan could only imagine how elated Clover must feel.

"Well, technically, she's not *supposed* to be on any, but it's only me in here, so I don't see why not. Hey, do you think you'll be able to volunteer this week?"

"I think on Tuesday or Thursday. I just have to double check schedules at work tomorrow night."

"Oh, okay. I was planning on doing Friday this week. I have choir practice every day after school this week until the concert on Thursday night."

"Oh, that's right!"

"And... it sounds like you may be free that evening? Would you want to come?"

"Of course. I'll definitely be there," Logan replied abruptly, surprising himself that he hadn't felt a need to stall and overthink.

"Okay, great. Well, hopefully I'll see you tomorrow morning?"

"Yes, sounds good. Tell Clover I say hi. Have a good night."

"You too, Logan."

Logan felt content as he sat back on his bed. Rough start to the conversation? Maybe a little, but he had recovered.

Things were getting easier the more he spoke with Kylie. There was nothing better than getting to spend time with her, even if it was just on the phone. He hoped she felt the same way.

CLOVER

I knew I wouldn't be going back to the dog room that night as I cuddled up to Kylie on her luxurious bedding. Everything on the bed had its own unique type of softness. The fluffy top layer was my favorite. At one point while I was lying next to Kylie, I heard her talking to Logan. I hoped he'd be coming over later.

The next morning, I was able to watch the day grow lighter through Kylie's window. I'd always woken up with the sun before my time in the dog room, and it was something I'd truly missed. I nudged Kylie since it was time to get up, but she didn't budge. I decided to go downstairs.

I pranced down the stairs, feeling refreshed. My head was clear and ready for a new day at Kylie's home. I stopped abruptly on the last step upon hearing stern voices coming from the kitchen.

"Wait, you mean you're not serious about giving this a real shot?" Mom asked. "I thought we agreed when we fostered her that it was with the intent of adopting her. We have two weeks to make this decision. I don't think you need to be saying all of this right now."

"Look, I would like for all of this to work out and for everyone to be happy, but I'm just not sure this family is ready for this much responsibility," the man replied.

"I can't believe you're saying this right now. Just give this a try, that's all I ask. We have two weeks with Clover."

I cocked my head after hearing my name. Maybe they were making my breakfast? But that was fun, and this didn't sound like a fun conversation.

"We'll see," the man said. "I'll give it more time like you're saying, but I'm just not sure about this."

"Not sure yet is fine. But yes, give it time. I really think this will be great. For all of us."

Their tone had become less tense, but it still seemed like they could benefit from petting a dog, even if it was just a temporary distraction. I walked into the room.

"Perfect timing, Clover. Let's get you some breakfast," said Mom.

Now they were speaking my language.

The man left carrying a fancy rectangular bag that he held with importance while Mom prepared my meal. While the food looked like what Miranda and others had been feeding me in the dog room, it had a much more appealing flavor, almost like the chicken scent that I could smell on Logan.

"Clover?"

It was Kylie.

"Clover! Hi, girl. I was worried when you weren't in my room this morning."

Kylie, hi. I'm right here. I was just hungry. Are you going to eat breakfast, too? What are we doing today? Can we go see Logan?

"You seem panicked," said Mom. "Everything's fine. Clover's here. Just fed her breakfast."

"Thanks, I'm not sure why I was so worried. Of course she's still here," said Kylie.

"Well, eat up and get ready for school. I know you have a big week with your choir concert coming up. How're you feeling?"

"Oh, good. We're going to be having rehearsals every day after school, but I'm feeling good about it. I'm just going to grab a granola bar this morning. I'm hoping to get to school early so I can see Logan."

"Ah, yes, the boy from the fair?"

"Yup, he's super nice."

"I see. Well, we know his father and um, well, just, be careful."

"Be careful? What does that mean? What's up with his dad?"

"He just… isn't the most sociable fella, I guess I'd say. He doesn't have the best reputation. He drinks. A lot. That sort of thing. Just not the ideal family we'd want you to be around, that's all."

"Mhmm. Well, that sounds unfortunate, but that shouldn't make you judge Logan. He's a great guy."

"I'm sure you'll make smart decisions. Have a good day, sweetie," said Mom as she kissed the top of Kylie's head.

I knew they'd been talking about Logan, so I got up, ready to head off with Kylie to meet up with him.

Kylie grabbed some belongings and headed out the door, leaving me behind. I sat down and barked. Clearly, this was a mistake. I was ready to go where she was going.

After a few minutes, I decided to lie down on my pillow in the living room to wait for Kylie. Mom tried to comfort me by scratching behind my ears and petting me on the head. I huffed and sighed as I wedged my head between my paws. If Kylie leaving without me had been an accident, she would've already come back. Did she go to see Logan? I didn't understand why she would've gone to see him without me. What was I going to do all day?

LOGAN

It was 7:22 a.m. and 34 degrees out when Logan pulled into his parking space at school. He knew the earliest he'd see Kylie was in another five minutes. He stared at his phone, unable to focus enough to do any one thing, so he sat back and closed his eyes and thought about how well things were going with Kylie. Then the Clovers appeared on Logan's shoulders.

You're doing so great, Logan, the good Clover said. *You've really been able to let yourself just be you and go with the flow. I'm so proud.*

Heh, but how long can you keep up that act, Logan? the other Clover chimed in. *Because it's not really you, is it? You don't know how to have a conversation with a girl, never mind kiss one or be someone's boyfriend.*

"Snap out of it," Logan told himself aloud as he lightly slapped his right cheek with his hand. "You've got this."

As Logan inhaled, he was startled to see a figure outside his door. Kylie? It was a woman, but he couldn't see who it was with his fogged car windows.

"You can't hang out in your car," the woman said with a muffled voice through Logan's closed door. "It's time to go inside."

It was a teacher. Logan glanced at the clock. It was 7:26. If he grabbed his belongings slowly, he would show the teacher that he respected the rules, but he'd still have a shot at seeing Kylie.

"Let's go. Time to get a move on," the teacher said as Logan got out of his car.

"Sorry," Logan replied. "Just gathering my thoughts before another big day at school, you know?" *What a stupid thing to say,* Logan thought. *Of course she knew. She's a teacher.*

"Okay," she said. "Well, time to get going now."

As if the message wasn't already clear.

"Yes, thanks," replied Logan with a forced smile.

He realized it didn't really make sense to thank her, but he didn't know what else to say. *Everyone liked to be thanked,* he thought as he tried to convince himself that what he said was fine.

Logan opened his backpack in his backseat and started to rummage through his belongings. He looked around his car to see if there was anything he could grab to make it look like he needed to make some serious decisions about what to take with him today.

He could see headlights coming his way through the window of his car door as he continued to move things around in his backseat. He smiled as the car passed, but it wasn't Kylie.

Figuring this morning just wasn't going to be his morning, Logan grabbed his bag and walked inside. The building was filled with voices of different groups catching up after the weekend. He could see Drew talking with some of his friends and gave them a quick nod but kept walking. He didn't feel like catching up with anyone but Kylie.

CLOVER

Mom had taken me out into the backyard after Kylie and Vicky left. The family had a tiny fenced-in area full of grass with a couple of large trees and a few plants. It was almost like a miniature farm. I sprinted through small piles of leaves and rolled in the grass. I wasn't able to go far, but I cherished this opportunity to be outside. I hadn't had enough of these moments lately.

When Mom called me inside, I realized she was getting ready to leave. She grabbed her things and didn't reach for my leash after she put her shoes on. I sat down and whimpered.

"Sorry, Clover. I have to go to work for a few hours. The girls will be home later, okay? I'm sure one of them will take you out for a walk. Be good."

When she closed the door behind her, I didn't feel as lonely as I thought I would. I was inside with an entire house to myself. This had never happened to me before. When I was alone on the farm, I was always outside or in the barn.

The first thing I decided to do was run. I took off for the kitchen and made multiple loops around the first floor. After a few rounds, I sprinted up the stairs, looked around quickly, then went back downstairs just as fast.

Food. What did we have for food? I'd noticed some scraps being deposited in a slender trash container in the kitchen the night before, so I decided to start there. As I stepped closer, I watched my reflection move on its surface. I'd experienced situations like this before on the street when looking at windows, but never with a trash container. It didn't keep me distracted for long. There was fresh food I had to get to.

As I took a step closer, my paw landed on a grooved pedal and the top of the container popped right open. It was an unexpectedly magical moment as the scents of food, new and old, started to pour out and fill my roused nostrils. These were the moments I knew I'd never forget. I jumped up to reach the opening and the entire container fell to the floor, creating an instant buffet.

I ate as much as I could before lying down to nap next to my mouthwatering mess. When I woke up, I decided it was time to venture upstairs again. I started with Mom's room. Judging by the scents and the room's contents, she appeared to share the room with the man who I'd come to believe was called Dad.

Their soft closet floor begged me to roll around on it, so I wriggled on my back every which way before sprawling out and lying down. Peering through the closet door, Mom and Dad's large bed enticed me to lie down on it and take another nap.

I woke up thirsty and went into their bathroom to get a drink of water from the toilet. As I made my way back to the closet, I felt a sharp pang of regret from my time at the kitchen buffet sting my stomach. My head lurched, then lurched again and again before I threw up onto the plush closet floor. I sat down and looked at the aftermath. I was proud of myself for not getting any on their shoes. People never seemed to like their shoes getting messed with.

I walked into Vicky's room next and snagged one of her stuffed animals. I took it to Kylie's room, jumped up on her bed, and slept until I heard the front door open.

"Clover?"

It was Vicky! I was happy to not be home alone anymore. I'd wanted to cuddle with someone ever since I'd thrown up in the closet.

I ran down to greet her and left her stuffed toy on Kylie's bed.

"Clover, there you are. How are you, girl? Did you have a good day? Were you a good girl? Let's get you outside."

When I came back inside, Vicky made her way into the kitchen.

"Oh my gosh. Clover!"

I hadn't known this girl for very long, so I wasn't sure if her reaction indicated that she was excited or unhappy. I opted to go with excited and ran to her with my tail wagging.

"Clover, bad. No. This is not good. We have to clean this up before Mom and Dad get home."

I was wrong. She was upset.

Vicky placed the trash container upright and took what was left of its original contents out to the garage. I guess she really liked to keep things organized.

When she was done, we finally got to cuddle on the couch. She spoke to me as I drifted off to sleep with my head in her lap. I was glad she didn't check the closet.

LOGAN

Logan called Kylie from his car as soon as his work shift ended Monday evening since he hadn't been able to catch up with her much at school.

"Hey, I'm so glad you called," Kylie said, sounding slightly frazzled.

"Hey. Everything okay?" Logan asked.

"Well, yes, and no. First of all, Jasmine was out sick today and she has a solo on Thursday, so the director asked me to take her place, and I completely bombed. I forgot all of the words about two verses in so then she had Rachel step in instead. I really wanted that, and I completely blew it. She gave a couple of other girls a shot too and said we could all try again tomorrow, but I'm sure she already has her mind made up."

"Oh, man. I'm sure tomorrow will be better," Logan tried to encourage as he fiddled with the keys dangling from his car's ignition.

"Thanks. I appreciate you believing in me. But... you've never even heard me sing, have you?"

Logan decided it was time to be bolder.

"Well, no. But I can just tell from your voice that you must be a beautiful singer."

"Ah, that's really sweet," Kylie said before pausing. "How was work?"

"Oh, pretty standard. It wasn't busy tonight, which was nice, so nothing crazy."

"Oh, good. What would a crazy night at River Ridge Chicken really entail, anyway?"

Kylie's playful tone calmed him and made him laugh.

"Hey, people can order some really weird things, okay? You'd be surprised by how many people request items that aren't even on the menu."

"Interesting. Okay, okay. Well, I'm sure you handle all of those situations with the utmost professionalism."

"Oh, yes. Of course. It's a truly classy place."

They both laughed.

"So, how's Clover doing?" Logan finally asked.

"She's good. Good. Yeah."

"I'm not sure I'm all that convinced by that answer."

"Well… today was her first day home alone, so I think we'd expect there to be some issues, of course. And, well, when my dad got home and went upstairs to his room, he found puke in his closet."

"Oh, no."

"Oh, yes," Kylie replied more dramatically. "And it wasn't just normal dog puke, either. There were some questionable things in it. Luckily, my dad didn't ask many questions, but Vicky told me that the trash in the kitchen had been knocked over and was all over the floor when she got home. So, my parents don't know that part, but I'm pretty sure that's why she threw up."

"Oh, wow. So is she okay?"

"Oh yeah. She seems great!"

Logan laughed.

"So, is your dad upset then?"

"Yeah, he definitely wasn't happy. He said that this is why people shouldn't live with animals, and if anything like that happens again that maybe things won't work out."

"Oh. Yikes."

"Yeah. It was just to my mom, but Vicky and I could hear them talking when we were upstairs. My mom didn't say much. Just told him he'd adjust, and everything would be fine, really. And I agree."

"Man, I'm sorry. I hope tomorrow goes better."

"I think it will. We tried to wear Clover out by playing a ton of fetch in the backyard tonight. A tired pup is a well-behaved pup they say, right?"

Logan pictured Kylie in her backyard playing with Clover. It was a picture-perfect vision.

"Sounds right to me. That was a good idea."

"Hey, I've got to get going. My mom is yelling upstairs to me about homework."

"Okay. I've got to get going myself. I'm glad I got to talk to you. Give Clover a scratch behind the ears for me. And hopefully I'll see you tomorrow."

"For sure. I'm going to set my alarm for ten minutes earlier than usual. I'll catch you in the parking lot."

After hanging up with Kylie, Logan sat back in the driver's seat, sighed, and smiled. Best conversation yet. He felt like his relationship was moving forward. But he was growing concerned about Clover. He hoped things would still work out.

CLOVER

All in all, I'd had a good day at Kylie's home. It was fun to roam around by myself, but I grew happier as each person arrived home throughout the day. I felt most at ease when Kylie returned home. And lying with her in her bed at night was the most relaxing and peaceful part of my day. I loved the warmth of her bed, the soft floor of her room, and how she talked to me like a friend. I did my best to listen thoughtfully and show her I cared.

"Okay, girl. You've got to make sure to get me up early tomorrow so I don't miss Logan on my way into school."

Miss Logan? I missed Logan. Was he going to come over? I hadn't found his scent in the house, so I figured that the chances of that happening were quite slim. I placed my right paw on her lap.

Kylie sighed as she leaned down to hug me. I closed my eyes to help soak in the love.

When it started to grow brighter outside the next morning, I stood on Kylie's bed and shook. My shake made a loud jingle again, just like it did when I'd lived on the farm. Kylie had adorned my neck with a new noisemaker the previous night. I hadn't always liked feeling constricted by them, but if it meant time at Kylie's home, I decided I could accept it.

"Go back to bed, Clover," Kylie mumbled.

I went over to lick her face since she'd said my name.

"Ah, man, Clover. What time is it anyway?"

Kylie rolled to her side and grabbed her phone.

"Oh, yikes. It's already 6:45. I've got to get going if I want a shot at seeing Logan this morning."

Seeing Logan? *Yes! Let's go see Logan!*

"Thanks for getting me up, Clover. You're a good girl."

Kylie gave me a quick pat on the head and started running from room to room. It was a fun new game that I hoped ended in breakfast.

At the bottom of the stairs, Kylie turned to me and said, "Okay, girl, I've got to go. Be good today, okay?" She scratched behind both of my ears. "Mom, you'll take care of her breakfast, right?"

"Yup, working on it now," Mom called from the kitchen. "Have a good day, honey."

The sound of fresh kibble made it easier to say goodbye to Kylie for the day.

Everyone continued to leave one by one, and I knew I wouldn't be taken to see Logan. While I loved spending time with Kylie, I liked it most when Kylie and Logan were together. And from what I could tell, it seemed they did, too. I figured it couldn't be much longer before we were all together again.

LOGAN

"Kylie, hi," Logan said as he got out of his car in the school parking lot on Tuesday morning. "It's good to see you."

"It's about time!" Kylie said half-jokingly with a laugh. "I've been standing outside in the cold long enough for the teacher over there to give me the side eye."

Logan chuckled.

"Well, I'm glad she didn't give you a hard time. You're definitely here early today!" Logan said as he threw his backpack over his right shoulder.

"I set my alarm extra early to make sure I got to see you."

"Aw, that's nice," Logan replied, hoping the cold air would cover as the cause of his increasingly red cheeks. "So how was the rest of your night with Clover?"

"Oh, good. She's so sweet. Last night, she just cuddled up against my legs at the foot of my bed and slept like that all night. She's been so good. Minus the couple of incidents yesterday, of course, but I think those are to be expected, right?"

"I would think so. I'm sure she'll have a better day today," Logan said as he started to mindlessly mess with one of his backpack straps. "How're you feeling about choir practice tonight?"

"Oh, definitely better. I think today will go well. Hopefully I can show Mrs. Henniker that I'm ready for a solo, but I'll also be okay if it doesn't work out. At least that's what I'm telling myself," Kylie said with a smile.

"Well, I'm sure you'll do great."

The couple was a few steps away from the school's entrance. Logan stopped playing with his backpack strap and slowed his pace.

"Hey, uh," Logan started, "have you thought about the upcoming Halloween dance at all?"

Logan clutched his hand into a fist unknowingly.

"No, actually. I honestly forgot that it was even coming up! With the choir concert, Clover, and, well, spending more time with you lately, I guess it fell off my radar."

"Ha, yeah, well you definitely have a lot of things going on. But… I was wondering… if you'd want to go with me."

Logan mustered all of his energy to maintain eye contact as he asked. He wasn't sure he could control the disappointment that would be strewn across his face if she declined.

"Yes," Kylie replied as she looked back at him with a smile, "of course."

Logan exhaled and his hands relaxed at his sides.

"I'd really love to," Kylie continued.

Logan was in awe of how effortless her answer was.

"Would you want to do the whole matching costume thing?" Kylie asked.

"Um, sure. If you want to," Logan said. "Definitely," he relayed more reassuringly.

"Okay, great. That would be so much fun. Yay! I'm sure we can come up with a great costume idea."

Logan watched as Kylie did a small jump and beamed with excitement while his mind went blank. "Yes, for sure," he replied.

"Oh and hey, are you volunteering tonight?" Kylie asked.

"I am, yeah." It hadn't been on Logan's mind today since Kylie wouldn't be volunteering with him, but he did still plan on going.

"That's great. Tell the pups I say hi. And please tell Miranda that things are working out really well with Clover if you see her. I've got to run, but I'll talk to you later."

"Okay, see you later."

Logan's grin remained as he walked toward his locker.

What am I going to do about this costume situation though? Logan wondered. Costumes weren't exactly his thing, but he was more than willing to compromise if it was important to Kylie. Maybe a costume would even help take some of the pressure off his first dance with a girl.

"Hey, man," said Drew as he rested his back against the locker beside Logan. "I haven't seen *you* in a while."

"Yeah, it's been a bit, huh? How's it going? Feeling ready for the choir concert?" Logan asked while sorting through his papers at the bottom of his locker.

"Yeah. Luckily, I don't have too much to prepare for like some others, so I'm just coasting. How're things with you? Still hanging out with the dogs and stuff?"

"Yeah, actually," Logan replied while continuing to rummage through his locker. "Headed there after school today. Kylie won't be there because of practice, but did you hear she's fostering the dog that I found at McCorley's?" Logan asked as he stood back up to face Drew.

"Oh wow, that moved fast. I'm assuming things aren't moving as fast for you though?" Drew asked with a sly grin.

"Yeah, no, things are good. I'm not sure if they'd meet *your* expectations, but they're good."

"Man, you're just so…" Drew started to say.

"What?" Logan interjected as he shut his locker.

"I don't know, man. You just have to get some experience, I guess."

"Well, I did ask her to the Halloween dance."

"Oh. Wow. Well, that's good. Good for you. What'd she say?"

"She said yes."

"Oh, good," Drew said again while nodding as he looked away.

"You don't seem all that excited," Logan said as his eyes narrowed.

"Oh, sorry. I just thought she might end up going with Billy. You know him, right? He's a senior. And also in choir. Billy Olympios?"

"Hmm…"

"It's no big deal, though," Drew said. "If she said yes to you then clearly there isn't anything going on there. I'm sure they're just friends."

"Right, yeah," Logan replied while looking down at the floor.

As the bell rang and Drew left for his first class, Logan couldn't help but doubt himself and Kylie's feelings.

Was her yes to the dance a real yes? Was it even worth it to start thinking about costume ideas? What was going on with Billy?

Logan tried to stifle his thoughts as he trudged to class.

CLOVER

I slept most of the day away downstairs after investigating all of the rooms, but on my best behavior. I wanted to make sure everyone was happy when they got home this time. I still hadn't figured out exactly what would and wouldn't make everyone in the house upset, so I decided to not do much of anything.

Vicky was the first one home again, and we cuddled on the couch before Mom arrived. Dad came home next, and I listened to him talk to Mom as she fed me dinner.

"So, you remember Samson and Bethanne, right?" Dad asked. "Samson from work?"

I saw Mom nod her head out of the corner of my eye.

"Well, I guess they've been talking about getting a dog."

"Oh, really? Well, that's good. They're fairly young, no kids. I'm sure a dog would be great for them," Mom said.

"Yeah, and I actually recommended that they go to Kiwi Canine Rescue, so they did yesterday."

"Oh good," Mom said. "Did any of the dogs seem like a good fit for them?"

"No, but they did sign up to be available for fostering if a dog comes along that matches what they're looking for."

"Well, that sounds good. Do you know what they're looking for?"

"That's the thing. It honestly sounds like they're looking for a dog just like Clover."

I had just finished my meal and was ready to go back out to the other room to rejoin Vicky, but upon hearing my name I chose to stay. They were both messing around with food on the counter, so I thought they might eventually have some scraps for me. Even though the kitchen floor was cold, I continued to lie down in order to stay within food-throwing range.

"Ah, I see. Hopefully another great dog will come along soon then! We're so lucky we found her. The girls just love her. I know we had a bit of a rougher day with her yesterday, but she'll learn."

"Will she, though? I know she was good today, or at least we think so since we haven't found any surprises yet, but I don't want to have to worry about coming home to a mess every day."

Mom huffed. "Oh Roy, you have *got* to be kidding. I don't want to have this conversation again. Clover did great today. Let's give this some time."

"I'm serious, Andrea. They're a lot of work, and they only cause destruction."

"You think our girls' love and devotion to a beautiful, kind, loving animal is destruction?"

"I'm not focused on that part."

"Yes, I think you've made that clear."

I regretted staying in the kitchen on the cold floor and wanted to leave, but the discussion seemed too intense to interrupt with my movement.

"Look, it's almost 6:00," Dad said. "I should add that I invited them over to stop by and meet Clover later. They said they could be over around 7:00."

"I can't believe you," Mom said in a louder voice as she dropped what she was working on onto the counter. "And what did you plan on telling the girls?"

"They don't need to know. I can just tell them that someone from work is coming by to pick something up."

"I can't believe you did this."

"They'll just come by for a little while. We can talk afterwards."

Mom resumed her work at the counter and a heavy silence filled the room. Mom was *not* happy. I went over to her and nudged her leg, but she didn't seem to notice. With the unnerving mood and lack of scraps, I decided to retreat to the living room. I hoped Kylie would be home soon.

LOGAN

Logan walked along the wall of the rescue's kennel room. He had to admit, the excitement of volunteering at the rescue was not at the level it once was with Clover gone and Kylie at choir practice.

He stopped as he passed the framed picture of Kiwi's nose print. He recalled Miranda's speech at orientation about the uniqueness of humans and dogs. While he couldn't remember everything she'd said, he did remember Miranda stressing how every dog and every person had something special within them that they could offer the world.

Surely, that doesn't include people like me. What about me is so different than anyone else?

Clover, on the other hand, had a personality that Logan had never encountered in another dog before. Something about her just made him feel understood and accepted by her. But Logan didn't feel he was necessarily unique to Clover. He could admit that she did appear to enjoy being around him, but she could be drawn to someone else just as easily. She was probably just grateful that he'd found her and given her some water when she was lost. He didn't feel that he had anything exceptional to offer Clover, or Kylie for that matter, that they couldn't find elsewhere.

"Hey, Logan. What's up?" Zoe asked.

"Oh, hey, not much. How's it going?"

"Good! It's nice to see you. Are you planning on staying a while today?"

"I am, yeah. Sorry about last time. What can I help with?"

"Well, the dogs in the back could use some time outside, and I can continue cleaning as they're taken out. Does that sound good to you?"

"Yup, sounds good."

"Is your sidekick joining you today?"

"My sidekick?"

"The girl. I can't remember her name."

"Oh. Kylie?" For a second Logan thought she might've been referring to Clover. "No, she's at choir practice tonight."

"Ah. Are you two… together?"

"Umm," Logan stalled as he bit his lip and looked to the floor.

"Oh, sorry. I didn't mean to make you uncomfortable. I tend to ask too many questions sometimes. Especially with people I like."

Oh. Whoa. Logan's eyes widened.

"And… I can be a bit forward, too," Zoe said with a smile. "Sorry."

"Um, all good. I, uh, am not necessarily with Kylie, officially, or anything."

"But you want to be."

"Yeah."

"Got it. I figured. I could see it. But thought I'd still check. Anyway, let's get going. We've got some dogs that are eager to stretch their legs."

"Right. On it."

Logan took the first couple of dogs outside and played fetch with them while trying to process what had just happened. It wasn't often that a girl straight up told him that she liked him completely out of the blue. What was going on?

As Logan brought the dogs back in, he caught himself looking at the nose print picture again.

"You're a real space cadet tonight, aren't you?" Zoe asked as she looked at Logan staring at the framed print.

"What? Oh, yeah, I guess so," Logan replied. "Hey, what are your thoughts on this picture? Do you really think everyone's unique?"

"Uh, well, if you ask me, people are more similar to each other than they are different, at least in my experience. Take me, for example. Here I am with my bright pink hair, and I could assume that was such a unique decision and hey, maybe I'm the only person with pink hair that you know, or some others know, but really, there are hundreds, probably even thousands, of other people out there with pink hair thinking the same thing. I don't always think that it's so much what makes you one hundred percent unique in terms of the whole world, but what makes you unique to the people in your life. That's easier to think about, for me at least."

"Yeah," Logan said with a nod. "Yeah, I like that, thanks."

"No prob. Now, back to work?"

"Ha, yeah. Back to it!"

CLOVER

I was so excited to see Kylie when she got home. She seemed tired, but happy, and I gladly accepted the love and affection she gave me upon entering. My tail wagged as she let me lick her face.

I was on high alert for falling food while the family ate dinner at their table. I'd been looking forward to this moment ever since breakfast. Sadly, not a single scrap fell to the floor. I went to my bed in the living room after dinner with my tail low and sighed loudly before lying down. I figured all of the exciting moments for the day had ended until I heard a loud ring and some noise at the front door a few minutes later.

"Who's that?" Kylie asked.

"Um, just a friend from work and his wife," Dad replied. "They're just here to pick something up, and I told them we were fostering a dog, so they were excited to meet her, too."

Kylie and Vicky snuck off upstairs as I watched Mom and Dad open the door.

"Samson, Bethanne, hi. You remember my wife, Andrea?"

Two people waltzed into the family's home, and I was too taken aback to bark. I stood up, unsure about what my next move should be. I sat down next to my bed.

"Of course. Hi, Andrea," the new man said.

"It's nice to see you again," said the new woman.

Were these nice people? Did they like dogs? Was anyone else going to be coming through the door?

I hadn't heard Logan's name mentioned all day, so I figured I wouldn't be lucky enough to have him make an appearance.

I let out a deep sigh.

"And this must be Clover," new man said.

I walked over to the group after hearing my name and was pleasantly greeted by the new people.

Were they going to sleep here, too? I wondered if there were other rooms in the house that I hadn't seen where these people stayed.

I looked over to Mom for any clues as to what was going on. She stood next to Dad and smiled, but it wasn't her usual smile. I went over to her, nudged her hand, and sat down. Something didn't seem quite right.

"Can I get you anything? Tea? Coffee?" Mom asked the newcomers.

"Oh, no, we're all set, thank you. We really just wanted to stop by for a few minutes to meet Clover here," the woman said as she reached out her hand toward me.

The man bent down and looked my way. "Yes, we don't want to impose. We know this was sort of last-minute, and we appreciate your willingness to have us stop by. Clover here is just a gem."

"She really is," Mom said.

Dad leaned in to speak softly to the new couple.

"Our kids… they don't know why you're here, so we're trying to keep things a little hush-hush. They're upstairs working on their homework."

"Ah, I see. Sorry, I didn't realize that," new man replied.

"Well, we can get going then. I think we've seen enough to know, really. She's truly everything we're looking for," new woman whispered.

I looked toward Mom, expecting her to speak next, but she didn't respond.

"Oh, good. Well, I'm glad you were able to come by and meet her," Dad said as he continued to speak in a soft tone. "See you tomorrow, Samson."

"Yes, see you tomorrow. Thanks for having us."

Mom waved to the couple as they left the house. Her strained smile had faded, leaving no signs of happiness, real or fake, behind. I watched as she stared blankly at the shut door, then decided to go upstairs.

I was surprised to see Kylie sitting in the hallway once I reached the top of the stairs. She got up and went to her room while motioning for me to follow. She gently closed her door, grabbed her phone, and jumped onto her bed. I snuggled up beside her, hoping to hear Logan's voice come from her phone.

LOGAN

"Hey," Logan said as he answered his phone in the backroom of Kiwi Canine Rescue.

"Logan, hey," Kylie said at almost the same time.

"How's it going? I have you on speaker, just so you know, while I finish working on some dog treats. I have to admit, volunteering hasn't been quite as fun without you and Clover."

The Clovers appeared on Logan's shoulders as he finished his sentence.

Okay, back off, said the bad Clover. *She may not actually even like you, remember?*

You'll be fine, trust me. Keep going and don't listen to that one, the good one said.

"Aw, it sounds like you're staying busy, though, so that's good. I… think I'm about to lose Clover."

"Wait, what?" Logan said as he stopped what he was doing, took Kylie off speaker, and picked up his phone.

"Did she run away again?" he asked.

"No, no. I, uh, just overheard my parents talking to some people that stopped by. It seemed like they came by just to meet Clover."

Logan took a deep breath to prepare himself for the rest of the story. It didn't seem like it was headed in a good direction.

Kylie started to speak even faster as she continued. "My dad said they had some visitors coming over to pick something up, but Logan, I don't think they left with anything. And they only talked about Clover. And they were talking softly after a little while. I just... I think my dad is trying to get them to adopt her or something. I don't know..."

"Okay, wow. Okay. Man." Logan started pacing and ran his hand through his hair before pushing his fingers into his temples. "Do we know if anything is really happening yet?" he asked.

"I don't... I guess I don't know anything yet. I just overheard all of this only a minute ago."

"Well I'm glad you called. So, hopefully this won't turn into anything. But I would think your parents would tell you if something was going to be happening with Clover, right?"

"Yeah. I would, too. But then again, we've never had a dog. I don't have anything to compare this to, I guess. Except the fact that we've never had a dog. I know I just said that, but what if my parents decided they just don't want a dog?"

"But Clover is so amazing. But of course you know that. Your family has two weeks to decide, though, right? So maybe this isn't anything to worry about. At least not yet. You should still have time with Clover before any choices need to be made."

"Right. I guess you're right. Nothing should be happening yet."

"Let me know if you hear anything else, but I'm sure things will work out. Did choir go okay today?"

"Yeah, actually. Mrs. Henniker actually gave me the solo. Jasmine is still sick, so she definitely won't be singing come Thursday. I feel bad, but I'm happy that I got the part."

"Wow! That's amazing, Kylie! That's so great. I can't wait to come to the concert." Logan paused. "If, you still want me there."

"Of course. I can't wait for you to be there."

Logan leaned against the wall and grinned.

After Logan and Kylie finished their call, Logan went to talk to Zoe.

"Hey, Zoe, when a dog is being fostered and under the two-week trial period, is another family able to foster the dog if the original people who are fostering change their minds?"

"Um, yeah, I guess so. If the original foster family changes their mind and another family is interested, then the dog can be fostered in the new home."

"And that new family would be able to adopt the dog?"

"Yes, they would be since the original family would no longer be interested, so the new family that's fostering would then get up to two weeks to decide if they wanted to adopt."

"Okay, thanks."

"How come? Is this about Clover?"

"Um, maybe. I'm really not sure yet."

"Okay. I can't imagine someone wanting to give that girl up. Hopefully that's not the case."

"Right. Hey, I've got to get going. It was good seeing you, though."

"Thanks for all of your help tonight. It was nice having you around."

"Thanks. Have a good night."

Logan put the hood of his sweatshirt up, then slid his slightly clenched fists into his sweatshirt pockets. The cold air swept across his cheeks and stung his nose on the dark fall night. Since Logan was feeling better about where he stood with Kylie after their conversation earlier, all he could think about was Clover.

CLOVER

I moved closer to Kylie on her bed. She smiled at me as I looked at her, but her eyes didn't shine like they normally did when she smiled. She seemed a bit happier since talking to Logan, but I could tell she was still sad.

She petted me absentmindedly before taking books and papers out of her backpack. I fell asleep quickly and woke up to Kylie turning the lights off and climbing into bed. She hugged me before we both drifted off to sleep for the night.

I dreamt about Logan that night. He was at the farm with me, Gloria, and Jake, sitting on the front porch in the sun. But suddenly Gloria and Jake were gone, and someone started walking in the driveway toward me and Logan. It was Kylie. I ran to her, and Logan followed to greet her. We walked in the corn fields together, and Logan and Kylie talked quietly while holding hands. I couldn't hear what they were saying, but they seemed happy. I was, too. The corn was endless in my dream, and we continued to walk and walk. Then I heard a loud noise and could see the corn rustling straight ahead of us. A tractor was coming toward us. I woke up before anything else could happen, but the noise from my dream continued as

I continued to lie in Kylie's bed. Was there a tractor in the house?

Kylie grumbled and rolled over. I pawed at her. If there was a tractor in the house, she had to get up.

"Clover, go back to sleep."

I pawed again. It was bright outside and there was a tractor downstairs. It was not time to sleep.

"Clover, it's fine. It's a blender. Just lie down. We only have a few more minutes before we have to get up."

She clearly wasn't understanding the sense of urgency here. Maybe she hadn't seen a tractor before, but I had seen what they could do, and they were powerful machines. Ones that didn't belong in a house. I jumped out of bed, went to her door, and barked.

"Okay, okay. There you go."

Kylie opened her bedroom door, and I ran downstairs to find the machine that didn't belong. I looked to the right quickly. The living room was clear. It sounded like the tractor was in the kitchen. I slid on the slick floor as I entered the room, but I didn't see farm equipment. Instead, I saw Mom and Dad with a noisy small contraption on the counter. It didn't sound as much like a tractor now that I was so close to it.

But I still barked.

"Clover, hey girl, it's okay," Mom said as the noise stopped. "Sorry if we woke you. We're trying to get healthier and we're starting with smoothies. Probably not as exciting for you, huh? No good scraps."

After breakfast, everyone left the house one by one, leaving me on my own again. I wasn't sure why I wasn't allowed to spend the days outside while they were away, but I was still content staying in the house. It still beat the dog room, and I knew everyone would be home again later.

LOGAN

Logan passed Kylie's car on his way to find a parking space at school Wednesday morning. He figured she must've been waiting for a while judging by the number of cars parked around her. Kylie was standing right outside Logan's car door by the time he turned his car off.

"Hey," she said.

"Hey, an early bird yet again!" Logan replied.

"I am. I had to make sure I saw you. I'm still rattled about Clover, and with the concert coming up tomorrow… I'm just, feeling a bit overwhelmed I guess."

"Well, I'm glad I get to see you. You're going to be amazing at the concert, and we'll figure something out for Clover. I talked to Zoe last night and…"

"Zoe?" Kylie asked abruptly. "The girl at the rescue?"

"Yeah," Logan said hesitantly.

"She has a major crush on you, you know."

"Oh, I…"

Kylie chuckled. "Already knew?" She smiled.

"I, uh, did actually kind of catch on to that yesterday."

Kylie raised her eyebrows as she looked Logan's way while they continued walking toward the school.

"Not that anything happened." Logan rushed to say. "I'm, uh, only interested in one person."

"I see," Kylie said slowly with a slight smile and squinted eyes.

"Yes, well, I hope so," Logan said as he stopped walking. Kylie took one more step, then stopped, too. "Since it's you," he said.

Kylie grinned. "Well, that's good because I'm only interested in one person, too," she said.

"Yeah?" Logan internally begged his face to remain a neutral color as he braced for Kylie's next words.

"Yeah. You," she said as she nudged his arm.

Logan realized he hadn't been breathing and attempted to inhale and exhale slowly without drawing too much attention to what he hoped was just a temporary respiratory impairment.

But what about Billy in choir? Why would you be interested in me over him? Don't you know other people like you? Why would you choose me?

Questions continued to rush through Logan's mind. He couldn't utter any of them out loud. He was too busy trying to maintain a smile and operate his lungs.

Despite his internal concerns, Logan decided to believe her. He had been open about how he was feeling, and she had too. He didn't want to ruin the moment. He felt like it was time to accept what he was hearing and stop worrying.

Logan and Kylie continued to smile at each other while standing in front of the school. He almost forgot where he was while he was caught up in that moment. It felt as if they were having a full conversation without even speaking.

"Well, I'm glad we both know where we stand," Logan said.

He resisted the urge to reach for Kylie's hand. Public displays of affection weren't allowed at River Ridge High.

"Me, too," Kylie replied. "I should get going, but I'll see you in class later."

"Sounds good," Logan said, hoping that moment would come as soon as possible. "See you later."

CLOVER

After a couple of hours of napping in the sun by a window in the living room, my nose drew me back into the kitchen. I'd continued to be fed morning and night, with food that still tasted better than what I'd been fed in the dog room, but my hunger was rarely satisfied.

I waltzed over to the kitchen trash container and sniffed. My mouth watered as I smelled the alluring mixture of the family's leftover meals from the last couple of days. A quick image of Vicky flashed in my mind from the last time she'd come home after I'd tampered with the container. She'd stood with her hands on her hips and no smile, clearly not a fan of my work.

She forgave me once, though, so, surely, she'd forgive me again.

I propped my front paws up on the container and knocked it over with what felt like fine skill and finesse.

The contents that spread across the floor were even better than before. I chomped on small pieces of boneless meat, lapped up a mysterious sticky liquid, and even consumed a few pieces of paper. I didn't typically dabble in paper products, but these had been soaked in multiple food sources and were uniquely delectable.

As I nudged the container to retrieve more of its tasty treasures, I heard an item crash to the kitchen floor behind me. Something rectangular that had been attached to a chord in the wall had fallen. It was flat, with a faint shine, and it smelled a bit like dad, but nothing like food. I watched as some of the liquids from the container started to approach it, but I ultimately decided to ignore it.

My stomach started to churn even faster than last time. I didn't want to toss everything up on my pile of delectable goods, so I turned to the item that had fallen and threw up on that instead. As usual, I felt better almost right away, but I still felt like lying down and taking a nap.

I slept on my bed in the living room, happy with how my morning had turned out. If the container was truly off limits to me, then they wouldn't have left it in the kitchen again. A dog should be able to eat at their own leisure. This was a luxury I'd missed during my time in the dog room.

As I slept, I dreamt about Logan and Kylie again. This time we were outside running over a hill to one of the most exciting scenes I'd ever seen: an entire field of trash containers. Logan and Kylie started pushing them over and spinning them around. I watched as the field quickly became covered in discarded goods. They laughed and smiled as I ran through the feast, unsure of where to start.

Before I had a chance to dream-eat my way through the field of fun food, I awoke with my snout nestled in a damp spot of drool on my bed.

Then I heard the front door creak. Someone was entering, but it was earlier than any of the other days that I'd been left alone. I wasn't sure who it would be. Could it be someone that wasn't supposed to be here? I wanted to bark, but I couldn't get the sound to escape by the time the door fully opened. It was Dad.

I didn't move. I watched as his gaze fixated on the trash in the kitchen. I started to wish it had been a stranger.

LOGAN

Logan walked into work expecting to see Seth but didn't. Wednesday nights were typically slower nights, so he wondered if the manager had decided to cut down on staffing for the evening.

"Hey, Sarah, do you know where Seth's at?" Logan asked. "I thought he was scheduled to work tonight."

"Ah, man, I guess you haven't heard," Sarah said as she replenished the stock of chicken buckets and lids. "Bill fired him this morning after he didn't show last night. I guess Seth had a family emergency come up, and even though we didn't even need the additional staff yesterday, Bill said he wouldn't tolerate that sort of behavior, as if Seth could control an emergency coming up. It's just ridiculous," she continued as she moved onto refilling the condiment packets by the takeout window. "I'm going to start checking out some other places around here to see if they need any help. I just can't stand working for this guy anymore. He's crazy."

Logan wanted to confront Bill, but also felt like it wasn't his place, even if he didn't agree with what happened.

"I can't believe that. Just like that… completely fired him," Logan said.

"Yup, Bill's already interviewing for his replacement. Thinks he can get someone in here by Friday."

"Oh, wow. What a fun time to start working here, during the busiest period," Logan replied sarcastically.

"I know, right? But Bill seems to think that if they can't catch on when it's busy, then they have no business working here."

"Yikes," Logan replied while shaking his head.

"Yeah, he's clearly not the one who's going to be doing the training. It's going to be rough."

Logan put on his gloves and approached the fryer to start working when Sarah continued.

"You should check the schedule, by the way. There have been a lot of changes."

"Okay, I'll check it later, thanks."

Logan operated slower at work that evening while he dwelled on his frustration with the new manager and wondered if Seth would be okay without a job temporarily. His thoughts shifted to Kylie later in the evening as he tried to play out how the following night could go. He pictured himself sneaking off to speak to Kylie before the concert began, smiling in the back of the audience throughout the performance, congratulating her once the show ended, and finally walking her to her car. He avoided even thinking about the idea of running into her family. There was no way he could prepare for that, he figured, so he'd just have to deal with it if it happened.

As Logan walked to his car after work, he realized he forgot to check the schedule like Sarah had suggested. As much as Logan wanted to head out, he decided to go back inside and check out the schedule posted outside Bill's door.

It looked like it was only for the next week, so there wasn't a ton that could've changed, Logan thought, but then he saw it. Tomorrow night. Thursday night. The night of the concert. He was scheduled to work.

Potential outcomes started running through Logan's mind as he stood with his shoulders slumped and mouth slightly ajar. He could act like he never saw the changed schedule and just not show up. If Sarah hadn't mentioned an updated schedule, how would he have even known to check? They were supposed to check it each shift now. He knew that. But he couldn't miss the concert. That just wasn't an option. He couldn't get anyone to switch with him either. The only two people that weren't scheduled to work were Seth, who had just been fired, and Daniel who was older and could never work on Thursday night due to other work commitments. There wasn't a way out.

Logan went back outside, sat in his car, and pulled out his phone. As much as he wanted to call Kylie first, he called Bill. He had to figure something out. He just couldn't work tomorrow.

"Hello?" Bill answered, sounding irritated already.

"Hi, Bill? It's Logan. Logan Greenfield. I, uh, just saw the schedule you posted?"

"Yes?"

"Well, I saw that I was scheduled for—"

"Oh, don't even try to tell me you want to change your shifts around. This was the only option that worked for the next week. You might've heard that I had to get rid of Seth."

"Well, yes. I did," Logan said as he started to absentmindedly play with a thread that jutted out from his steering wheel. "I, uh, actually wanted to talk to you about that. I think it would be worth it to bring him back. At least for a few days until someone new is trained."

"Are you kidding? There's no way I would have him come back. Or anyone that disrespects my schedule like that. I schedule the times. Everyone needs to adhere to them. It's as simple as that. There's really no need for this shift swapping and unavailability business that people are trying to pull. Even you. I'm surprised by you right now. I thought you were one of my best workers."

"I would like to think that I am. This isn't about my work ethic, though. I just can't… I'm not available to come in tomorrow."

"I see. You don't want to work. And you want me to bring back a disrespectful worker. I think I've heard enough. If you don't show up tomorrow, you're fired."

"I—"

Logan heard silence on the other end and looked at his phone to see if the call was still connected. It wasn't. Bill had hung up.

"Okay, new plan," Logan said aloud to himself. "I quit."

CLOVER

To say Dad was upset upon seeing the display I'd left in the kitchen would be an understatement. I didn't quite have the right word for what I witnessed from him.

First, I heard him let out a yell that escalated enough to make me cower and stay on my bed. The sounds he made weren't words. They sounded wild.

Then he yelled Clover. My name. I'd never heard it uttered so harshly and loud.

I figured he wanted me to come, but I was terrified. As I stood up from my bed, I couldn't help but pee a little before slowly looking around the corner. He was holding the flat object that had fallen from the counter. If that's what he was upset about, I hadn't played a role in it. I'd only wanted to eat the contents of the container. I didn't want what he was holding. But it had smelled like him, so part of me understood that it must've been important to him and that's why he was so mad.

I whimpered. I wished there was a way for me to tell him that it had fallen on its own.

I spent a long time outside after Dad's outburst. At first, it was an enjoyable change to be outside, but after running laps, I'd been left with little to do.

I sat by the door and waited. I could see Dad through the glass door, staring at his rectangular toy and occasionally beating on it with his hands. Sometimes people and dogs liked the same things, like food, stuffed toys, and people. But it was times like these that really made me think about just how different people were from dogs. I could never understand why that particular object was so important to him. I didn't have anything similar of my own that I could try to give him. But if I had, I would've tried.

Mom came home next, and I caught her eye immediately as she opened the front door. I wagged my tail as she opened the door to let me back inside.

I'm so glad to see you. Please pet me and let Dad know that I didn't make his toy fall. I was just hungry. That thing had a mind of its own.

Mom petted me slowly as she listened to Dad rant about what I could only assume was his beloved sleek rectangle. I stayed in the living room as she entered the kitchen.

"Oh my gosh. Look at this place," Mom said.

My panting slowed and my muscles relaxed slightly as I realized she wasn't going to yell like Dad had.

"Look at this *place*?" Dad said tensely. "Look at *this*. My laptop! Completely ruined. I had everything on this. Everything. Never mind the fact that I'd only had this for a couple of months. This cost me, *us*, thousands of dollars. And it's all gone because of a dog? We're just… I can't… this has gotten out of hand."

"Roy, clearly Clover didn't ruin your laptop on purpose. The trash strewn everywhere? That, I can say, appears to have been purposeful. But the laptop? It looks like it was just caught in the crosshairs. I'm not sure the kitchen was the best pla—"

"I'm going to call Samson later. See when they can take Clover. We're just not a dog family."

"Roy, I need you to give this more time. We all love Clover. I know it's a lot to get used to, but she's an amazing, loving, brilliant animal. And she loves us, too."

"We can't have a dog running around destroying our house every day. How is that feasible?"

"We can help control that. We can move the trash to the garage. We can make sure our valuable electronics aren't accessible. That's on us."

"I'm still calling Samson later. At least they really want a dog."

"Roy, we did, too. We *do*, too. I know you're struggling with this, but there are three other family members here that should get a say. And Kylie's big choir concert is tomorrow night. She's been practicing for weeks. She has a *solo*. You can't take her dog away at the same time."

"Fine, they'll find out after the concert. In the meantime, Clover better behave."

LOGAN

When Logan got home from work, he flung his jacket on his bedroom floor and tossed his backpack on his bed with carefree movements and a broad smile. He was feeling liberated after deciding to leave his job at River Ridge Chicken. He'd saved enough money for him to comfortably last months without a job, but he knew he shouldn't take advantage of that if he didn't have to. He would start asking around and applying for a position at a different restaurant or another business that coming weekend. But he had no plans to return to River Ridge Chicken. Logan made a mental note to check in with Seth, too, but first he had to do something for Kylie.

Logan needed to find his mother's necklace with the paw print and clover charm for Kylie. He wanted to let her borrow it for her performance the following day.

After rummaging around in his closet for a few minutes, he found the small wooden box engraved with his mother's initials that held the necklace. The box looked smaller than he'd remembered, but the necklace looked the same. Logan hadn't looked at it for years. He had learned at a young age that things happened in life that were completely out of his control, and he tried to avoid being reminded of this fact as much as possible.

As Logan continued to look at his mother's necklace, he heard his phone ping to alert him to a new text message. His heart started to beat faster as he saw it was from Kylie.

Hey Logan. I hope you had a good night at work. I won't be able to catch up with you tonight. I came home from choir practice to find my parents fighting and I'm just exhausted. I'm excited to see you tomorrow. Hopefully I catch you in the morning. Good night.

Logan's heart went out to Kylie in that moment. He felt terrible that she was feeling so off and hoped she'd be better tomorrow for her big solo at the concert. The necklace would be that much more important if she wasn't feeling supported by her family right now. He wondered if they had been fighting about Clover based on what Kylie had told him recently. She couldn't lose Clover. He couldn't, either.

Logan started to text Kylie back. *I'm sorry to hear about your rough night. I'm here if you want to call me later.*

Logan thought twice and deleted his last sentence. *I'm sorry to hear about your rough night. I'm excited to see you tomorrow. Give Clover a scratch behind the ears for me. Good night. Sleep tight.* He started to second guess the addition of "sleep tight," but he sent the text before he could dwell on it any longer.

Thanks. You too, Kylie texted back almost instantly.

Logan held his phone and closed his eyes. Everything would be okay, he told himself, while thinking about Clover, the concert, his relationship with Kylie, and his new jobless status.

He dug out his homework from his backpack and sped through his assignments in record time. He was ready to drift off to sleep and see Kylie in the morning.

CLOVER

Things weren't much better when Kylie arrived home the night of Dad's destroyed rectangle. Mom and Dad had eventually stopped talking to each other and the energy in the house had turned tense.

The dinner I witnessed was different than previous nights. The family didn't sit at the table together to eat the same meal. They went in and out of the kitchen at their own leisure, taking different food and eating it on their own without much conversation. Vicky spent most of the evening in her room after dinner. Kylie did the same and I decided to join her, unsure of when the unsettling feeling that had spread throughout the house would dissipate.

I hoped she'd make Logan's voice come out of her phone, but she was focused on papers and books all evening instead as we sat on her bed.

I did get a nice scratch behind my ears after her phone made a noise, though, and it reminded me of the way Logan used to pet me. I missed Logan. I was starting to wonder if I had to run off to find him again. I was torn since I loved being with Kylie and her family, but I was starting to feel like I wasn't always welcome. It was confusing to think about. I let out a screechy yawn before closing my eyes and falling asleep while Kylie finished her work. I snuggled up to her when she climbed into bed later after shutting off her lights.

"Everything's going to be okay, right, girl?"

I nudged her hand, and she started petting me.

"You're going to be able to stay here and everyone will be happy?"

Even though Kylie was speaking softly, the sadness in her voice was unmistakable.

"I can't imagine losing you. I know that's why Mom and Dad aren't speaking tonight. It's so stupid. It's only been a couple of days. You're our dog."

Kylie hugged me as she sniffled. I licked the salty water off her cheeks and cuddled closer to comfort her. I knew that each day didn't always turn out as expected, but from what I'd witnessed in my life so far, I'd come to find that things had a way of working out and leading to events, places, people, sights, sounds, and food that weren't always imagined. After taking off from the farm, the last place I'd pictured myself was cuddled up to a girl in a new home, with new friends and new experiences that had continuously brought me joy over the past few days. Even my time in my closet in the dog room, which wasn't ideal, had led me to Kylie and Logan, and I was grateful. But this evening's events and corresponding energy in the household had me starting to feel like it still wasn't time to completely let my guard down. Things may not be as permanent as I'd hoped.

It took longer than usual for me to fall asleep that night, but as Kylie and I continued to reassuringly snuggle with each other, I was able to relax enough to drift off to sleep.

LOGAN

Logan was surprised to see that the sun had already risen as his phone's message ding woke him up. Kylie was asking if he was on his way. The message's timestamp read 7:35 a.m. He couldn't believe he'd slept in. Logan had always woken up when he needed to. He swore he had the ability to tell himself what time he wanted to be awake by and his body would follow his internal command. But that wasn't the case this morning.

He sprang to his feet and quickly grabbed some clothes, hoping the shirt he pulled from the pile on his chair wasn't one he'd already worn that week. He hadn't always been the best at keeping tabs on things like that, but now he had someone else he thought of when making decisions like this. Logan gave the shirt a quick sniff and decided it was good enough for the day.

Without any time for breakfast, he grabbed what was left of a box of crackers on the counter and was on his way out the door.

He tossed his backpack in the backseat, started his car, and texted Kylie back before leaving. He apologized and explained he wasn't going to make it in time to see her.

Later in math class, Logan snuck a note to Kylie in the seat in front of him, then held his breath as he noticed the teacher approach.

"And what do we have here?" Mr. Apollo said as he raised his eyebrows and tilted his head.

Logan's face heated up right away.

Mr. Apollo snatched the note out of Kylie's hand.

"What should I do, what should I do?" Mr. Apollo asked as he started pacing at the front of the room with the folded note. "Should I… toss it? Give it back? Maybe read it to the class…?"

Logan remained completely still in his seat and blinked as if he was in slow motion.

"Ah, I'm just kidding with you," Mr. Apollo said, suddenly less intense. "I get that some teachers would have a field day with this, but I never understood that sort of thing, really. Why should I get such a kick out of your personal lives?"

He handed the note back to Kylie.

"I respect my students' privacy, but I also ask that you respect our time in this class, so I do ask that you wait until after the bell rings to read your note," the teacher finished.

"Yes, of course," said Kylie softly.

"Sorry for the distraction, Mr. Apollo," Logan chimed in while briefly making eye contact with the teacher.

"All good, Mr. Greenfield. Thank you for helping me teach this important lesson to the class. See, we can learn about more things than parabolas and quadrants, right? I like to think that I teach a mix of math and practical life lessons," he mused with arm movements that reminded Logan of a band director.

Before the teacher could continue, the bell rang, and the students rushed out faster than usual.

"Hey, I'll walk you to your next class," Logan said to Kylie in the hallway.

"What, are you crazy?" Kylie asked with a giggle. "Your next class is completely on the other side of the building from mine."

"It's okay. I haven't been late to that class once and Ms. Zeplin likes me."

"I didn't realize you were such a rebel," Kylie said as she nudged Logan's arm.

"Sometimes you've just got to do what you've got to do," Logan replied while also thinking about how he would effectively be quitting his job tonight by not showing up. "I wanted to make sure I caught up with you. I can't believe I slept in this morning."

"I know! What's gotten into you, Logan Greenfield? First, you don't show up to school a half hour early, and then you go and risk being late to a class. What's going to be next, a bank robbery?" Kylie asked.

"I guess my rebellious side is paying a visit."

"I truly thought I'd never see the day, but if there's going to be one, I'm glad it's today," Kylie said as she looked over at Logan with a sweet grin.

He swore he saw a twinkle in her eye.

"I just wanted to make sure you were having a better day than yesterday. Your text last night had me a little worried."

The couple slowed their pace as they walked.

"Yes, I'm better, thanks. Just trying to focus on the concert tonight."

"That's smart. I'm so excited for you tonight. You're going to be amazing."

"Thank you. I'm excited, too. Especially since you'll be in the audience."

Logan's face heated up instantly, but he smiled as he attempted to accept Kylie's kind words.

"Well, here we are," Kylie said as she arrived at her next classroom. "Thanks for walking with me. I'll see you tonight."

"Yes, for sure, can't wait."

The pair stood in the hallway momentarily. They knew there were too many teachers around to make any sort of physical contact, so they smiled at each other while Kylie giggled softly before turning to go into her classroom, clutching her books tightly in her arms.

CLOVER

Once everyone had filtered out of the house the next morning, I busied myself in Kylie's room. I'd never been in trouble in that room and felt it was the safest location for me after yesterday's events. Even with everyone out of the house, there was still a heaviness in the air that made me feel slow, like I was walking around with a bag of dog food on my back.

I snooped under Kylie's bed but didn't find anything compelling. I propped my paws up on the top of her furniture and looked around at the flat surfaces covered in Kylie's things. There were small tubes with sparkles and tiny trinkets that were probably important to her, but nothing that I could find an immediate use for, so I let everything be.

After continuing to explore Kylie's room, I retired on her plush bed and placed my head on her pillow. It smelled the most like her in that spot, and I felt my muscles relax as I continued to lie there.

I barked and quickly rose to my feet upon hearing the door to the house open downstairs. I hoped it wasn't Dad again, but then I smelled him. I exited Kylie's room and walked cautiously down to the living room to find him. I feigned excitement by wagging my tail a couple of times upon seeing him, hoping he wouldn't make the same sounds as yesterday.

"No mess today I see, Clover. Or was that not on your agenda until this afternoon?"

He didn't sound like he had the day before, so I took that as a good sign. I would've felt better if he petted me, though.

He gave me a quick pat on the top of the head, then busied himself in the kitchen. He took out my bag of food and my bowls and set them on the counter along with a couple of my toys. I wasn't sure what he was doing.

A few minutes later, there was a knock on the door. It was the woman who had stopped by earlier in the week.

"Bethanne, thank you for coming over," Dad said as the woman entered.

"Of course, we're so excited to have Clover in our home."

I walked over to her after she said my name. She bent down to scratch behind my ears and smiled at me when I sat down. I wished she was Logan or Kylie. I didn't find her very exciting. Her scent was faint and smelled clean. She didn't smell like food, and most certainly not like any of my favorites like chicken, but I did appreciate the attention. She seemed nice; she just wasn't for me. I wondered how long she'd be staying and if the man who was with her last time would be joining her soon.

"I have to make this quick because I've got to get back to work, but I put Clover's belongings together on the counter in there. I can bring them to your car if you'd like."

"Oh wow, you didn't have to do that. We have food and everything else she should need at home ready to go already."

"Okay. Well, at least take a couple of those toys. I think she likes them. I'll throw the rest in the garage later."

"Okay, I'll grab some toys. And maybe this bed for her, thanks."

Much to my surprise, Dad then grabbed my leash. I wasn't expecting to go on a walk while he had a visitor over, but I was too excited to show any hesitation. I sat down so Dad could attach my leash to me.

"Oh wow, she's so patient while you get her ready," the woman said.

"Yes, I guess she's always been pretty good at that," Dad said as he ruffled the top of my head.

"I'm impressed."

Dad handed the woman my leash.

"Well," she said, "I guess we'll call you if we have any questions, but I'm thinking it will be smooth sailing. She's such a sweet girl."

"Yes, I'm sure everything will be fine. Enjoy. And thank you again for coming by."

Dad gave me another quick pat on the top of my head before the woman opened the door. I guessed she was just here to walk me. What a nice surprise. I happily followed her out the front door, ready to show her around the neighborhood.

Instead of continuing to the sidewalk, the woman opened the back door to her car. A car ride before a surprise walk? I was game. I jumped in, ready to find out where we'd be going and who we'd be seeing.

LOGAN

After school, Logan had a couple of hours to spare before he had to be back for Kylie's choir concert.

Now that his irritation with his soon-to-be-former manager, Bill, had waned, he figured he should call him to give him a heads up that he wouldn't be in tonight, or ever again. But first, he wanted to talk to Seth.

As Logan walked to his car to make the calls, he was surprised to see Drew sitting on a bench outside the school.

"Hey, aren't you supposed to be inside prepping for tonight's concert?" Logan asked as he approached Drew.

"Yeah, I'm going to be headed back in in a minute, but I was hoping to catch you first," Drew replied as he stood up and ran his fingers through his hair.

"Oh. What's up?" Logan asked, trying to sound indifferent, but nervous that Drew was going to drop more bad news about Kylie.

"I, uh, wanted to fill you in on something I saw happen at choir practice last night."

Logan held his breath as his throat felt like it was starting to close in on him.

"With Kylie, that is."

Logan stared at Drew with full focus, waiting, not blinking.

"I think… well, I'm pretty sure, actually, that I was wrong about her and Billy. There's nothing there, I guess. At least not on Kylie's end."

Logan let out the little bit of breath he'd been holding in and blinked his eyes in disbelief. He had prepared himself for more bad news, so he was shocked at the words coming out of Drew's mouth. Logan didn't reply as his body returned to a normal state. Drew continued.

"Last night, Billy tried to ask Kylie to the Halloween dance and Kylie flat out told him no and that she was going with you."

Logan continued listening, still on high alert in case the conversation went in an unwanted direction. Drew didn't typically deliver positive news about girls to him.

"Not only that," Drew continued, "she actually went on to say something like how she was only interested in you, period."

"Oh. Wow," Logan replied, still in disbelief.

Logan knew he and Kylie had talked about these reciprocated feelings when they were alone, but he didn't know she'd be comfortable enough saying anything to others, especially to someone who was interested in her.

"I know. I was shocked, really. I mean, I'm happy for you, don't get me wrong, I think I'm just surprised. Ever since

I've known you, you haven't even gone on a date, never mind had one of the prettiest girls in our class interested in you. So, I guess what I'm also trying to say is I'm sorry. I didn't realize she was so into you."

"It's okay," Logan said. "I might be just as surprised as you."

"I'm sure you can't be too surprised. You guys have been talking a lot, right?"

"Yeah, I guess," Logan said as he diverted his eyes, not wanting to say too much.

"Well, I don't know how you did it, but good for you. I'll be coming to you for advice soon enough probably," Drew said as he patted Logan on the shoulder.

"So what about you?" Logan asked. "Do you have a date for the Halloween dance yet?"

"Nah, man. I don't think I'm going. It seems pretty lame."

"I'll take that as a no," Logan said with a laugh.

"Man, who's taking the cheap shots, now?" Drew half-joked as he scuffed the ground.

"Ha, yeah, I guess so. I'm sure you'll find someone, though," Logan said. "If you want to go, that is."

"We'll see. I've got to run. I should probably show up to at least some of the practice before the choir dinner," Drew said as he started walking backwards toward the school. "But good luck, man. It seems like you're on the right track!"

Logan wished Drew good luck before heading to his car, feeling surprisingly confident and energized after their unexpected conversation.

Logan called Seth while he sat in his car and was sent straight to voicemail.

"Hey man, it's Logan. I heard what happened with Bill the other night and I still can't believe it. I'm sorry. That shouldn't have happened. I wanted to give you a heads up, though, that I'm quitting. Tonight. I'm calling Bill as soon as I'm done leaving this message. Just wanted to let you know. Hopefully we can catch up soon."

Logan hung up and called Bill right away.

"Hello," Logan heard from the other end with a sigh.

"Hi, it's Logan Greenfield."

"Again? Yes?"

"I won't be in tonight."

"You've got to be kidding. If you don't come in tonight, say goodbye to your job. I warned you about this."

"I know. And I'm prepared for that. And," Logan continued before Bill could get a word in, "I would suggest you reach out to Seth to see if he can come in. He's a good employee and he may just be willing to accept an invitation to come back. I'm sure this isn't what you want to hear, but—"

"You're right. It isn't."

Logan couldn't believe he was actually giving a speech to Bill, but now that Logan was leaving, he didn't fear him quite as much. This was going to be his only shot at saying some of the things he really wanted to say.

"I just… things come up sometimes. I know his job was important to him."

"Well, thanks for the courtesy call, I guess. I've got to go figure out what I'm doing about tonight now that we're short-staffed. Again," Bill replied, clearly agitated.

"Okay, and I'm sorry, I—"

Logan realized he was talking to dead air. Bill had already hung up.

He let out a deep breath. While he was technically unemployed now, he was thrilled to not have to work for Bill again. And he had just received further confirmation that Kylie was definitely into him. For the first time since he started high school, Logan was feeling like things were starting to fall into place for him.

CLOVER

I wasn't in the car with the visiting woman for long before we came to a stop. She turned to me in the backseat and said the word "home," but we hadn't made our way back to Kylie's house. It wasn't home. Did Dad know he'd let me leave with a liar?

When we exited the car, I pulled the woman in the direction we'd just come, trying to show her that home was that way.

She took me inside the new house instead. It smelled like her and the visiting man from the other night: clean and soapy, but with faint hints of food. Sounds echoed in the entryway, the ceilings stretched high, surfaces around me glimmered, and nothing appeared out of place. It didn't seem like a place for a dog to be visiting. I sat down, respecting the order of the home, and looked up expectantly at the woman, hoping this was just a quick stop before we got back to our walk.

"Welcome home, Clover," the woman said as she hung up her coat. "I'm so excited. I can't wait for Samson to come home later. He's going to be thrilled."

I cocked my head. I wasn't sure what she was trying to communicate. If we weren't going on a walk, I wanted to get back home.

"Let me show you the kitchen, girl. I can show you your matching food and water bowls, both propped up in a cute little holder."

I wagged my tail and followed the woman into her kitchen. I lapped up the water in the bowl as quickly as I could.

"You're a thirsty girl, I see. That's good. Stay nice and hydrated because we'll be going on a run later."

The woman petted me. She still seemed nice, but I wanted to understand what we were doing. She grabbed a bottle of water from the fridge before walking into the next room.

"And here's your kennel, Clover."

She pointed to a rectangular structure with crisscrossed metal bars.

"Go on," she said as she pushed her arms forward. "Give it a whirl. It's supposed to be the perfect size for you."

I approached the structure hesitantly and sniffed the entryway. Was this a cage? I could tell she wanted me to go inside, but I wasn't all that interested. She gave me a soft nudge and my front paws entered the confined area. It was an odd structure. It was restrictive due to its size, but I still felt quite exposed with the openings in its walls and ceiling. While I hadn't noticed any unsettling difference in temperature since entering this house, I suddenly felt chilled.

I stood still as I watched the woman shut the cage door with me still inside.

"I've got to head out, but I'll be home later and so will Samson. Be good."

There was the word "home" again. Was she going back to Kylie's? If she was, why wasn't I going with her?

I sighed and decided to lie down while resting my head on my front paws. I let out a quiet whimper as I thought of Kylie and Logan. They wouldn't keep me in this tiny space if they were here. I didn't know how long I was going to have to lie in here. I didn't understand why I couldn't be free to explore. Nothing smelled all that appealing in the house, so I surely wouldn't have been able to get myself into too much trouble. I let out a huff and hoped Kylie would come and get me soon.

LOGAN

Logan paced backstage at the school while he waited for the students in choir to finish their warmups in the practice room. He'd tucked his mother's necklace in his pocket, ready to present it to Kylie on loan for her concert.

Choir members started to filter in backstage. Logan stood to the side to wait for Kylie.

"Hey, man. What are you doing back here?" Drew asked as he approached Logan and gave him a quick hand slide and fist pound.

"I, uh," Logan started.

"Just wanted to wish me luck, right? That's so very nice of you. Thanks, man," Drew joked as he nudged Logan's shoulder.

"Oh, yup, here just for you. Wishing you all the best of luck, Drew," Logan feigned.

"Nice, man. That was *super* convincing," Drew replied with an eyeroll. "Don't worry, your girlfriend will be here any second, I'm sure."

"She's not—"

"Your girlfriend. Yes, of course. Right. Well, have fun in the audience. I hope you enjoy the show."

"Yes, and really, good luck, man. Catch you later," Logan said.

Drew walked toward some other choir students while Logan tuned in to a nearby conversation while waiting for Kylie.

"Um, didn't she already turn you down, dude? Why put yourself through that again?"

Logan glanced at the person speaking. It was a student named Graham talking to Billy, the guy that Drew had warned Logan about. The guy that had been turned down by Kylie in what Logan had understood to be in a very clear and direct way.

"Yeah, but you know girls can never make up their minds. They don't know what they want. I'm going to try again after the show," Billy told Graham.

"Whatever. Do what you want I guess, but at some point, you may need to learn to accept reality," Graham replied.

"You'll see. I feel good about it," Billy said.

Logan started breathing quicker and turned away so that the boys didn't notice him.

Should I say something to Kylie? Should I be worried? Logan wondered.

"Logan! Hey!" Kylie exclaimed as she approached Logan backstage.

"Hey, Kylie." Logan smiled.

Kylie approached him quickly and appeared like she was going to hug Logan, but she suddenly slowed down and backed up a step. "I'm so glad you're here," Kylie said with a grin.

Logan noticed how beautiful she looked. Kylie didn't typically wear much makeup, but she appeared to have some on tonight and he found her to be striking with accented eye lashes and deep red lips. He caught himself staring at her mouth briefly before he spoke again.

"Me, too. You look beautiful," Logan said, the words spilling out of his mouth without giving them a thought.

"Aw, you're so sweet, thank you. I'm so nervous. But what a great surprise that you're back here. I wasn't expecting to see you until after the concert."

"Yeah, I, uh, actually—"

"Oh, hold on one second," Kylie said. She turned toward another student. "Heather, hey. I want you to meet Logan." Kylie turned back to Logan. "Logan, this is my best friend, Heather."

Logan took a breath, relieved by the distraction. He wasn't sure if he was going to mention Billy or give Kylie the necklace, so additional time to ponder was more than welcome.

"Heather, hi. I think we might've had history class together last year. Ms. Hannigan's class?"

"Oh, yes. She was quite the character, huh? But I will say I sure learned a lot. It's nice to see you again."

"Yeah, same," Logan replied.

"I've got to go get something from the practice room," Heather said. "Did you want to come, Kylie?"

"Uh," she looked at Logan before looking back to Heather. "I think I'll stay back here."

"Okay, I'll see you in a few," Heather said as she walked away.

"Sorry to interrupt you," Kylie said. "I just really wanted you two to meet. I've kind of been talking about you a lot lately."

Logan could feel his face grow warmer.

"I see," he replied. "Hey, I, um, have something I want to give you. For the concert. Just temporarily. It was actually my mother's."

Logan reached into his pocket to grab the necklace while Kylie looked on in anticipation, her eyes focused on Logan's hand retrieving the item.

"It's a necklace. I thought it might give you some good luck for your solo tonight."

"Oh, Logan, wow."

"Not that I don't think you're going to crush it tonight without this or anything, because I do. But these charms have new significance to me with Clover now, and I figured you'd like the charms too, so I thought you might be interested in wearing it tonight."

"Yes, of course. Wow, it's beautiful. That's so thoughtful. Thank you, Logan."

The pair smiled as Kylie clasped the necklace around her neck with ease. Logan let out a deep breath, relieved. He wasn't sure he could have kept his hands steady enough to help her if she'd needed assistance.

"I love this. Thank you. I honestly feel so much less nervous already," Kylie said with a smile while examining the necklace's charms. "I'm not sure if it's just because of you or if this necklace has some sort of magical powers," Kylie said with a laugh.

"It's probably the necklace," Logan replied with a half grin while he looked at Kylie.

He felt like they were having an entire conversation while only looking into each other's eyes again.

"Thanks for coming back here. I'll take good care of the necklace, I promise. Thank you again," said Kylie.

"Of course. I'll be rooting for you. See you afterwards."

Billy was a lost thought in Logan's mind as he walked away with a grin.

CLOVER

It took me a moment to get my bearings after waking from a nap in the cage in the clean house. I could smell the visiting man from the other evening at home before he fully opened the front door. I remained lying down while staring at the door, ready and unexcited to see his figure enter the building.

"Clover, girl, how are you?"

His voice was high-pitched and sweet, and if I didn't know any better, it could be mistaken for kind. But I figured he was involved in keeping me trapped in this structure, so I wasn't thrilled to see him. I sighed while he took off his jacket and placed it on a peg on the wall. He didn't seem to be in a rush to get me out as I watched him enter the kitchen.

He reappeared after a couple of minutes to unlock the door that had been keeping me encaged. I was relieved to be out, but I was reluctant to act too excited since I shouldn't have been kept in there in the first place.

"Are you sleepy, Clover? You don't seem very energetic. Do you need to go outside maybe?"

Outside? Yes. Was I finally going to get to go on a walk? I'm sure Dad was expecting me to be home by now. I was willing to let the cage situation slide if I ended up going on a fun adventure.

The man didn't seem to be dressed to spend time outside, but new people surprised me sometimes, so maybe he was just as ready as I was.

He let me out the back door of the house into a grassy area. It was quite similar to Kylie's backyard. Things smelled similar, too. I knew I wasn't too far from home.

I relieved myself and then ran around for a minute before looking back toward the door to see if the man was coming. Maybe he was putting his shoes on. I sat down and waited patiently, but he didn't come. After another minute, he finally opened the door, but called to me instead. I cocked my head. I wished I could call him instead. I barked.

"Clover, come. Now."

His voice had grown stern. I walked toward him, unsatisfied with the continued series of events since I'd arrived at this place. I wasn't ready to go inside. I didn't want to go back in the cage. Surely, Kylie and the rest of the family would be expecting me at home soon. What if Kylie was already home? It was still light out, so I figured I hadn't missed her yet, but I still wanted to be there when she got home.

My head hung low as I walked through the door and passed the man. I chose to lie down in what the woman had called their living room, although the room didn't seem very lived in. The furniture looked pristine and uninviting. The floor didn't have crumbs or any fun surprises that I'd be interested in sniffing or snacking on.

"Clover, time to go back in your kennel. I have to get back to work. But I'm happy to see that you've settled in so well."

I watched as the man walked over to the cage. I could let one instance of being kept in there go, but if this man was making me go back in that confined space again already, I couldn't understand why. I stared at the man as he pointed, and I finally let out a whimper. Didn't he know I didn't need to be kept in there?

"I know you misbehaved when you were at Roy's. And I get it. You were left alone with nothing to do. I wouldn't be mad at you for that. But I'm also not willing to provide an environment for you to get into trouble. So, into the kennel you go. Come on, Clover."

The thought of calling upon my body to lift itself up and proceed to the cage exhausted me. Surely, if I just kept lying down, he could see how tired I was and let me be?

"I see. Well, let me see if I can change your mind."

He retreated to the kitchen again. I didn't even feel like getting up to investigate. I knew he wouldn't be preparing a tasty snack for either of us.

"Here. Want a treat? Come get it. Come on."

The man threw a small piece of food into the cage. Someone must've told him that I couldn't turn down food.

I'd like to think that I'm a fairly clever dog, but if I truly was, I probably wouldn't have gone for that treat. Part of me knew I'd be locked back in the cage, but my nearly constant hunger overruled any reliable logic.

"Gotcha," he said as he closed the door. "Good girl. We'll see you later. Be good."

LOGAN

Logan found a place to sit in the back of the auditorium as the lights flickered which seemed to indicate that the show would be starting soon. He'd never been to a choir concert before, never mind one to support a girl he was into.

Logan saw Kylie's parents and sister enter the auditorium and find a spot to sit close to the stage. Kylie's mom had a bouquet of flowers in her hands. Logan scanned the room and noticed that others had brought bouquets, too.

Is that a thing? People are supposed to bring flowers? Logan wondered.

Logan's right leg bounced up and down as he started adding up the bouquets he saw, then doubled the number thinking he was probably seeing less than half and then thought about how many people were probably in choir. According to his rough calculations, at least half of the students would be receiving a bouquet.

Logan didn't have time to run out and find a decent flower arrangement, so he stayed put. Soon after, the lights dimmed and without the bouquets in sight to point out Logan's potential mistake, he decided to move on from his concern and shift his focus to the stage. A bright light shone on a microphone stand and three tiers of bleachers stood behind the microphone in a U-shape.

After a quick introduction from the choir director, the students filtered out row by row. Kylie was one of the last to enter and stood in the front row, close to the middle, but far enough to the side so Logan could still see her when the director stood in front. She was easily the most beautiful person in the room. The way the lighting graced her face made her look angelic. Logan caught a quick glimmer from his mother's necklace around her neck. His muscles grew less tense as he sat back in his chair.

After a few songs, Logan was surprised when the director announced a ten-minute intermission. He'd noticed that some audience members had held programs, but he wasn't sure where they'd gotten them from. *Did people print them out before they came?* Logan wondered.

As people filtered out for the intermission, Logan decided to stay where he was. He snagged a program from a now-vacant seat in front of him and scanned to see when Kylie's solo would take place. He saw her name highlighted as a soloist for the second-to-last song for the evening. Only four more songs until Kylie's big moment.

He'd always thought that choir was for super dorky students until he'd moved and started going to River Ridge High. It seemed like more of the "cool" kids were involved in choir there than he'd expected. The whole idea of getting together and singing still didn't appeal to Logan, but he started to understand why some of the kids might be into it as the night went on.

Logan had planned on placing the program back on the seat he'd taken it from, but he held onto it instead. He wanted something to remember this evening by. The concert was a big deal for Kylie, and he also felt like it was a big step for their relationship. Logan wanted to make sure that Kylie knew that he'd be there to support her for moments like this.

When Kylie sang her solo, he realized he'd never heard a song sung so beautifully. His eyes were wide and focused as he sat entranced by Kylie's flowing voice. It was like no one else was on the stage as Kylie sang. In Logan's mind, everyone else in the audience had disappeared as well. He couldn't be sure that Kylie knew where he was sitting, but he felt like she was looking at him the entire time and singing straight to his heart.

At the end of the song, he stood and clapped with the most enthusiasm he'd ever shown for a performance. He'd just witnessed the most captivating singing of his life and he was ecstatic that it came from the person he was falling for more and more with each day.

The concert ended with a fun blend of upbeat holiday songs that left everyone cheering. Logan beamed at Kylie as he stood and clapped again. He was surprised at how much fun he'd ended up having at the concert. He couldn't wait until the next time he heard Kylie sing.

CLOVER

I continued to lie alone in the metal structure that I figured must really be for animals smaller than me. I thought back to my most similar experience stuck in a tiny space. It was during my time at the dog room. While I certainly hadn't loved that time and shivered at the thought of its cold floor and walls, there'd at least been enough people around to keep things a bit more interesting. We were talked to, taken outside, and fed. And even though I wasn't able to see the other dogs in their rooms while I was in my closet, I always knew they were there. We were all experiencing the same situation together, even though we were separated.

In this cage, I had no one and nothing. Not even a toy to keep me entertained. I was stuck. And alone. And ready to get back to Kylie and everyone at home.

When the couple returned to the house later, I stood up, not from excitement, but in need of getting outside to relieve myself. They spoke to each other in excited tones as they took off their jackets and scarves. I whimpered.

"Ah, Clover," the woman said. "How are you doing, girl?"

I pawed at the contraption's door. *Get me out of here.*

"She seems pretty anxious. Do you think she's okay, Bethanne?"

"I'm sure she's fine. She probably just has to go out," she said before approaching me. "But good girl for not having an accident in your kennel. Nice job."

The way this woman spoke to me reminded me of the way some people spoke when they were around a baby. As soon as she opened the cage door wide enough for me to squeeze through, I rushed to the back door and ran outside.

I felt better after a few moments in the fresh air, but soon realized just how hungry I was. It was dark out and definitely past my normal dinner time. Would I be brought back home for dinner? Did these people even know I had to be fed?

I looked back at the doorway and didn't see any sign of either person inside. I decided to walk along the perimeter of the fence. As I approached a part that branched off of the house, I noticed a piece of fencing that wasn't in line with the rest. Then I realized why. It was a door.

I ran as fast as I could through the opening, then quickly sniffed the front yard to get my bearings. I felt confident that I could find my way back home to Kylie. I took off in the direction the woman had taken me, ignoring the pangs of hunger in my belly as I embraced my getaway moment. It was time to go home.

LOGAN

Logan wasn't standing far from Kylie's family as he waited for her in the school hallway after the concert. He turned his back to them and pretended to busy himself with his phone in case they noticed him. He felt slightly cowardly but speaking to Kylie's family presented an opportunity for the night to take a turn for the worse, and he didn't want to take that chance. He just wanted to see Kylie.

Logan could overhear Kylie's parents as he scrolled through his phone, not even registering anything he was looking at. Kylie's sister had run off to talk to some friends, leaving her parents alone.

"I don't want to tell her anything until we get home," Andrea said.

"Right, I agree. I won't say anything yet," Roy replied.

"Well, really, there shouldn't even be anything to say," Andrea said with frustration. "We were supposed to give this more time. But we can't get into that right now. I don't want to ruin Kylie's big night. Her performance was outstanding. She's got to be the best singer in the school, don't you think?

She could probably even get a scholarship if she continues to pursue this."

"She was quite good. And I also don't want to take away from that, but Clover just wasn't working out for our family. At least not right now. Maybe we can consider a dog again in a few months."

Logan stopped pretending to scroll through his phone as he focused on the words he was hearing. *Could Clover really be gone?*

"I'm not sure you'll ever be ready," Andrea replied before lowering her voice. "But really, I just don't get it. I know you're not *used* to having a dog around, but I thought you liked Clover."

"I did, actually. I really did. When Bethanne left with her, I have to admit I kind of missed her." He paused and cleared his throat. "But, again, it was the best thing for us."

"I knew you'd regret making such a rash decision," Andrea said, her voice growing louder before she lowered it again as she continued. "I know you have a lot going on at work. Do you think you were just looking at this as an opportunity to make a change? Like, overseeing something that you could truly control?"

"Oh, stop," Roy replied with a huff. "You sound like a therapist. Let's not bring my job into this. It just wasn't going to work out with Clover, end of story. Now look, here comes Kylie. I think this conversation is over."

Logan regretted overhearing Kylie's parents talk about Clover and hoped it somehow didn't really mean she was gone. He picked his phone back up and stared at it mindlessly. When Kylie came over to him, Logan looked up and was captivated by her radiating energy and beauty.

Kylie let out an excited squeal before hugging Logan. He avoided making eye contact with her parents as he hugged Kylie back.

"Your performance…" Logan started to say as they took a step back from their embrace. "I can't even put into words how captivating it was."

"Aw, thanks. That's nice of you. It was exhilarating being up there," Kylie said, beaming with pride as she clutched the bouquet she had received from her parents.

Logan's mother's necklace caught his eye as he listened to Kylie's energized reaction to the concert. His smile grew as he realized how truly happy he was in this moment to be there supporting her.

Luckily for Logan, Kylie's parents had started talking to Drew's parents, so they hadn't come over to bother them. What he had overheard about Clover crept back into his mind. If Clover was really gone, he felt obligated to somehow get her back.

"I've got to head home, but you were absolutely amazing tonight. Congrats," Logan said.

He thought about apologizing for not bringing her flowers but decided against it. The last thing he wanted to do was take away from her happiness by adding any pressure on her to make him feel better about his lack of concert-attending etiquette.

"Thank you so much. I'll call you later," Kylie replied as she turned away to join some others from choir.

Logan left, eager to come up with a plan to get Clover back. He was grateful for the clues he'd overheard, and even more grateful for successfully avoiding Kylie's parents for the evening.

CLOVER

The air had grown crisp as I ran down the side of the street, positive I was going in the right direction. I recognized some of the scents and scenes from walks with Kylie's family over the past few days. There was a statue of a miniature person with a tall pointy cap in someone's yard that smelled of other dogs' urine. I remembered barking at the figurine the first time I'd seen it, unsure if it was going to move. I'd decided it had clearly shown its submission to other dogs by smelling the way it did, so there probably wasn't any reason to worry.

I turned a corner and saw cars driving by, so I turned back around to remain on a quiet street. I knew the road with the cars wasn't the right route to get back to Kylie. I continued on and passed a house with flags waving from its walls, another memorable landmark from my recent walks. I was getting closer.

I could hear a rumbling noise behind me and turned to see what it could be. It was a car in the distance. I was excited at the prospect of the car being filled with Kylie and her family. Or could it even be Logan? We seemed to run into each other on occasions like this. While the possibilities for the car were appealing, I still decided to hide behind a bush in the flag house's yard. I couldn't take any chances since the car could also be transporting the clean couple with the cage. I remained behind the shrub until the car passed. I felt like I'd made the right decision.

After coming out from behind the shrub, I was lured into the backyard of the flag house upon smelling one of my favorite scents: an assortment of discarded goods. I wasn't let down as I scoped out their yard. Sitting against the side of their house was what I could only imagine would be a scrumptious dinner for myself encased in a large trash container.

This container didn't have quite as many edible products as others I'd experienced, but I was able to scrounge out a few tasty pieces of mysterious food and gnawed the meat off of some discarded bones. It was enough to satisfy my hunger and allow me to regain focus for the rest of my trip back home. I didn't want to be away from Kylie any longer.

I passed a few more houses before I heard another car behind me. I hid behind a bush again. This time I was at a house I was less familiar with. This car was driving faster. It reminded me of Logan's. Could it be? I peered out from behind the bush but couldn't see the driver.

I ran to see if it was Logan, but the car didn't slow down as I ran behind it, struggling to catch up. If it had been Logan, he surely would've stopped to get me. I strolled back to the sidewalk as the car drove out of sight. Then I sniffed the air.

It smelled like I was getting closer. Then I saw it. Kylie's house was just across the street. I'd made it home.

LOGAN

Logan stretched out on his bed when he got home after the concert, unsure of what he could do about Clover. His phone rang and he bit his lip upon seeing that it was Kylie. He figured she must have found out about Clover being gone. He closed his eyes as he answered the phone, bracing himself for the conversation they were about to have.

"Kylie, hey," Logan said somberly.

"Hi. You won't believe what happened when we got home."

Logan felt a lump grow in his throat. He'd expected Kylie to sound more upset after learning about Clover going to a new home, but instead, her voice sounded fast paced and almost cheerful.

"Um, what happened?" Logan asked, still waiting to hear the disappointing news about Clover.

"We pulled into the driveway, my dad opened the garage door and was about to drive in, but then you won't believe who I saw sitting outside."

"Who?" Logan asked with a thoroughly furrowed brow at this point.

"Clover!"

"What?"

"Yeah! Clover. She was sitting right outside our front door."

"What? How?" Logan let out a breath.

"I really don't know. I didn't want to ask too many questions with how weird my dad had been acting lately. I really thought he was trying to get rid of her."

"Right. Wow. I can't believe she was at your front door."

"Yeah, I have no idea how she got there. I was still so excited after the concert that I just opened the car door while the car was still moving and ran out to her and hugged her. She didn't seem all that cold, so I don't think she could've been outside for too long. But I really don't know how she got there. Maybe my parents accidentally left her out in the backyard before they left for the concert? But she would've been much colder, right? So, I have no idea. I was just so happy to see her."

"Wow," Logan said as he sat back on his bed and took a breath. "What did your parents say?"

"Well, I didn't really hear their initial reaction because I was too busy running to Clover, but my mom seemed excited too, but also confused. We got Clover inside and my parents talked in another room. I did hear my dad eventually say something along the lines of 'I guess this is where she's meant to be,' and my mom was quite happy for the rest of the evening, so I think whatever had been going on with them and Clover is over now."

"Wow, I'm so relieved to hear that," Logan said, still in disbelief, as he shook his head and ran his fingers through his hair. "I'm so happy for you all." Logan paused. "So, when's the next time I'll get to see Clover, anyway?" he asked. "I feel like it's been forever."

"Want to go on a walk with us after school tomorrow, then we can go volunteer? Or do you have to work tomorrow? I can't remember."

Logan had planned on job hunting after school, but the possibility of hanging out with Kylie and Clover was much more appealing.

"Nope, I'm free. That all sounds great."

"Perfect. Well, I'll see you tomorrow, then. Thanks again for coming tonight. That really meant a lot to me. And oh my gosh. I just realized I still have your mom's necklace on. I'm so sorry I forgot to give it back to you."

"Oh, that's all right. It's in good hands. And you did amazing tonight. Congrats on such an amazing performance."

"Why, thank you, thank you," Kylie replied with a fake British accent. "I'll get the necklace back to you tomorrow. I know how special it must be to you."

"Thanks, sounds good. See you tomorrow," Logan replied before hanging up and clutching his phone to his chest.

CLOVER

I hadn't waited outside at the door long before my family came home. Kylie had jumped out from the car and seemed both excited and relieved to see me. They must've been out looking for me. I wondered if Dad had explained the mix-up with the lying lady.

When Kylie and I went inside, all I wanted to do was snuggle up with her on her bed. We stayed downstairs for a while, but as soon as we were upstairs, I jumped up on her bed and cuddled with her as she talked excitedly to Logan on the phone. I flipped my head backwards and nudged her whenever she stopped petting me.

When I woke up with the sun the following morning, I jumped out of bed and stretched, feeling rested and better than I had in days.

I pranced down the stairs, and Mom let me outside right away after a quick pat on the head. It was even colder than the previous night. I looked back at the door to see Mom standing there waiting for me. I was so thankful to be back home.

I came back inside following Mom's call and sat down at the bottom of the stairway, waiting for Kylie to come barreling down and run out the door as she usually did. I was ready to spend the day by myself relaxing after the unpleasant events and uncertainty of the day before.

The girls left the house quickly, leaving Mom and Dad talking in the kitchen.

"So they'll be over in a few to drop off Clover's things?" Mom asked as she fed me my breakfast.

As much as I enjoyed eating people's leftovers while adventuring, it was also nice to have a hand-scooped meal at home.

"I'd like to make sure she has her bed before we leave for the day."

"Yes, Samson should be here any minute with all of Clover's belongings," Dad replied as I chowed down my meal.

"Great. And they're okay with us keeping her?"

"From what I could tell, yes, but we didn't talk a ton. I guess we'll get a better idea when he gets here."

I looked up at Mom upon hearing a knock at the door. I wasn't thrilled at the idea of visitors coming just one day after being taken. I considered running upstairs but decided to stay in the kitchen.

I smelled the now familiar man's clean scent as Mom opened the door.

"Samson, hi. Thank you so much for coming over," Mom said as the man smiled, and Dad walked over. "I know the circumstances are pretty unique. And surprising," Mom continued.

"Yes, I would say so. But it seems like this is where Clover's meant to be, and Bethanne and I would never want to interfere with that. I actually already called Miranda at the rescue, and we plan on stopping by there again next week to see if we click with any of the dogs we met before and meet any new ones. I'm sure we'll find the right one soon enough. And in the meantime, we're happy that you and Roy changed your minds."

I watched as Dad retrieved the items that the visiting man had been holding. My items. But I stayed put in the kitchen, not wanting to draw any attention to myself. If the man didn't notice me, he couldn't take me.

"Yeah," Dad said, "it was really just me that had to come around, honestly. But even I can't deny that Clover belongs here now. And the family loves her. She really does seem at home here."

"I would say so. The first opportunity she had to get back here, she took. That's a dog that knows what she wants if you ask me. I'm glad she's here," the man replied.

"We are, too," Mom said. "Thank you again for bringing Clover's things over this morning. I'm going to go check on her. Please excuse me."

"Yes, of course," the man replied. "I have to get going myself. Best of luck with Clover. Roy, I'll see you later."

"Yes, see you soon," Dad said as he shook the man's hand.

I stood up when the man left, feeling more at ease, and walked over to where Mom stood in the kitchen. It was still early in the morning, and we'd already fended off a visitor. I felt powerful. And still a bit hungry.

LOGAN

Logan had missed seeing Kylie before school and now felt like the day couldn't pass any slower as he moved from class to class. The anticipation of spending the afternoon with Kylie and getting to see Clover again had overtaken Logan's thoughts. He wasn't typically one to draw, but he found himself trying to sketch dog nose prints in his notebook during his afternoon classes. He thought again about how the nose print was supposed to represent uniqueness, but he still couldn't figure out something about himself that made him any different than anyone else.

When the final bell rang, Logan stopped at his locker then rushed outside to meet Kylie. He'd only seen her briefly in math class, so he was eager to spend more time with her. And he couldn't wait to see Clover again. He'd missed her so much.

"Logan! Hey!" Kylie shouted as she stood just outside the school's entrance.

"Hey!" Logan replied.

Logan was tempted to give Kylie a hug as he approached her but reminded himself that they were still surrounded by everyone at school. He stuffed his hands in his pockets and smiled at her.

"It's so good to see you," Kylie said. "This day could not have gone by any slower."

"Oh, I know! What was up with that?"

"So you experienced it too, huh?" Kylie asked with a laugh. "I guess we were both looking forward to seeing each other."

Logan still admired how Kylie seemed to easily say what she was thinking, a quality he felt he lacked.

"Yes, I think so," Logan said. "And I can't wait to see Clover! I still can't believe what happened after the concert last night."

"Yeah, same here. Just sitting there, outside, waiting for us to get home."

"Yeah, it seems pretty crazy."

"Definitely not something I'm going to question. I'm just so happy she's home."

"I bet," Logan replied as he noticed the sunlight reflect off of his mother's necklace.

"Ah, your necklace," Kylie said as she unclasped it with grace. "I figured it was best to keep it on until I got it back to you," she continued as she handed it back to Logan. "Thank you again for letting me borrow it. That really meant a lot."

"Of course. It looked great on you," Logan replied, thinking maybe there'd come a time where she could wear it permanently.

Kylie grinned.

"So," Kylie said, "I was thinking I could drive us to my place to get Clover and then we could head to the rescue together after? Then I can bring you back here to get your car when we're done at the rescue."

"Okay, sure," Logan said. "Sounds like a plan to me."

Logan could already feel his hands starting to get clammy in his pockets.

"The more time together, the merrier, I figured," Kylie said.

"I agree again," Logan said with a smile.

It was a short drive to Kylie's house from school, but it was long enough for Logan to repeat, 'stay calm' and 'breathe' about 100 times in his head before they arrived. They hadn't talked much in the car. He thought Kylie might also be a little nervous since he noticed how focused she was on the road out of the corner of his eye. There hadn't been any hand holding in the car, so when their hands brushed together as they both reached for the radio controls, the jolt of energy Logan felt made him pull his hand back from surprise. Logan watched as Kylie's eyes widened. He figured she must have felt something similar.

"So you're not a fan of this song either, huh?" Logan asked.

"Oh, no, I was actually reaching to turn the volume up!" Kylie said as she laughed.

Logan could feel his face grow rosier as he sank back into his seat.

"It's okay," Kylie said. "It's not like our tastes in music have to be the same if we're going to hang out together."

Logan smiled and focused on his breathing again.

When they pulled into Kylie's driveway, she mentioned that her parents wouldn't be home and that she'd run in to get Clover.

"She's going to be so surprised and excited to see you, Logan."

"I'm excited, too. I can't wait to give her a big hug and take her on a walk. I can't believe it's been so long since I've seen her. She probably thought I disappeared."

CLOVER

Kylie came home before anyone else for the first time since I'd lived with her. I ran over to her to be petted and noticed a faint but familiar and luring scent on her right away: Logan. I didn't think my tail could wag any harder, but it started to. I missed Logan so much. Where was he, and how could I see him? I sat down and looked up at Kylie.

"Need to go out, girl?"

Kylie let me out in the backyard, and I squatted to relieve myself as fast as I could. I was eager to get back inside to see what was going to happen next.

"I've got a surprise for you, Clover," Kylie said to me as I darted back in the house. "We're going to go for a walk!"

"Walk" was one of my favorite words. I couldn't wait to go for a walk. I just hoped she meant it was with her. Last time a walk was arranged for me, I was dognapped. I wasn't looking for that to happen again.

"And we have a fun visitor for our walk today!"

Visitor? No. I whimpered.

"Trust me, you'll like this surprise. Let me just get my scarf and let's get your harness and leash."

Kylie draped my harness over my neck and buckled it up. It looked like she was coming with me, and no visitors had entered, so I was feeling less wary. My tail returned to its usual state of wagging.

As soon as Kylie opened the door, I could smell him. It was Logan! I ran so fast that I pulled the leash out from Kylie's grasp, but she didn't yell. I think she knew I wouldn't go far.

I rushed over to Logan and jumped up on him. I'd never jumped on him before and it wasn't something I typically did, but this reunion was special. I couldn't help myself. He bent down, and I licked his face. His chicken scent seemed to have faded since I'd last seen him, but he was still amazing Logan, and I loved him. I couldn't believe we were all together again.

I could tell Logan was radiating with joy upon seeing me, too. He kept saying my name and telling me he missed me.

I missed you too, Logan.

Kylie looked on and laughed as we continued to get reacquainted.

After we'd all settled down, we walked around town, passing some of the places I'd stopped at the night before. I pulled slightly as we passed the house with the fun trash container in the backyard, but Logan redirected me and kept me on the sidewalk. I knew I'd get fed later, so I was happy to oblige and keep walking. Maybe we could stop there another day.

We continued to pass new scents and houses on different streets and walkways. I smiled the entire time as my tongue hung happily from my mouth. I hadn't felt so at peace since the day we'd spent at the odd farm. I was happiest when we were all together.

Logan and Kylie talked and laughed quietly as we walked. Logan held my leash the entire time, which let me know he wasn't going anywhere. As long as my leash wasn't dragging on the ground, Logan was still there.

I missed the moment it happened, but by the time we arrived back home, I saw Logan's hand intertwined with Kylie's. They were probably trying to keep each other warm. It had grown darker since we'd started our walk around town.

Kylie knelt down and spoke to me. "We're going to go see Miranda at the rescue this evening."

I wagged my tail.

"I know you must remember that place, huh? But I'll be home later. You'll have to say goodbye to Logan for now."

Kylie stood and then Logan knelt down next to me. The mood had shifted, and I could sense some somberness from Logan. Was he leaving? I wasn't ready for the fun evening to end.

"It was so good to see you, Clover," Logan said as he looked into my eyes. "I'd missed you so much."

He wrapped his arms around me, and I buried my nose in the crevice of his arm, inhaling his fading chicken scent as I closed my eyes.

"I always thought that dogs didn't really like to be hugged," Kylie said.

"I don't think they typically do," Logan said with a laugh. "But as we know, Clover isn't your average dog."

"True. And even if she likes hugs, she probably doesn't want to be embraced by just anyone."

"Exactly. Kind of like people," Logan said as they laughed.

"Are you not a hugger, Logan?"

"Um, no, not really, I guess."

"I didn't think so," Kylie said as she chuckled before turning toward me. "All right, girl, it's time for us to go. Everyone else should be home soon and they'll make sure to feed you. I'll see you soon."

I licked Logan's face before Kylie took me back inside. I knew I'd see Logan again, but it was still hard to be separated.

LOGAN

"Man, I can't believe how much I love that dog," Logan said to Kylie as they got into her car to head to Kiwi Canine Rescue.

"It's adorable," Kylie replied. "You can tell she loves you just as much."

"Thanks for having me over. I'm so glad I got to see her. And I'm so happy things seem better with your dad and Clover at home. Just in time for Halloween."

"Ah, right, Halloween. I'd been so focused on the choir concert that I almost forgot Halloween is next week."

Logan was relieved that some of the earlier tension in the car ride over had died down after their walk together. The conversation started to flow much easier for Logan on the ride to the rescue.

"Are you going to dress Clover up for Halloween?" Logan asked.

Kylie chuckled. "I'm not sure. I haven't even thought about that really. I think more importantly, we need to decide what we'll be dressing up as for the dance."

"Right, that's only a week away," Logan replied, trying to play it cool and ignoring the internal countdown clock he had flashing in his mind. *Only seven more days!*

"Maybe Miranda and Ben will have some costume ideas for us."

"Yes, that's a good idea. Let's ask them tonight," Logan replied as he slid his hand toward the center console, closer to Kylie.

"You're funny," Kylie said with a smile while keeping her eyes on the road.

"What?"

"Each time we're together, it's always like you're unsure of what to do around me at first, but then you come around."

"Takes me a bit to warm up, I guess," Logan replied while trying to sound as confident as possible.

"It's cute. It's fun to guess when you'll try to make a move."

"Ah, so my hand moving over was me making a move?"

"Well, I thought so," Kylie said before she paused. "Was it not?" she asked with a grin as she took Logan's hand.

Logan's face grew warm, but he smiled back. *There she goes again with her bold statements,* Logan thought. He liked when she called him out. He felt like there was a good balancing act going on.

When the couple walked through the front doors of the rescue, they were greeted by Miranda.

"Ah, well if it isn't my two favorite high school volunteers," Miranda said as she stood up from behind the front desk and greeted Kylie and Logan.

"Do you say that to all of your volunteers?" Logan asked.

"Well, I guess I'd be lying if I said I didn't greet all of my volunteers in a similar fashion. Especially the ones who come back after their first few days. You'd be surprised at the turnover we have after people have volunteered for more than a week or two. It's not always what people expect it to be, I guess. Maybe we need a new orientation video or something."

"Well, this place helped me and my family get the dog that I've waited for all my life, so I'll gladly volunteer here for as long and as often as I can," Kylie said.

"Aw, that's sweet. How's Clover doing?" Miranda asked while stepping back behind her desk.

"She's great. We just took her out for a walk before heading here," Kylie replied.

"Oh, good," Miranda said. "I know she loves a good walk. And if it was with the two of you, she must've been beyond thrilled."

"Yes, she seemed pretty excited," Logan replied.

"Good, good. So what are you both looking to do tonight?" Miranda asked.

"Whatever's needed," Kylie said.

"Okay. Well, we have a new dog that doesn't seem to be enjoying his time here so far. A little Chihuahua named Boo. You'll see him as soon as you walk in. And you'll probably hear him right away, too. So if you wanted to spend some time with him, either in his kennel or outside, or even both, that would be a great way to start. Otherwise, Zoe and Tim are also back there, and I'm sure they'll have a list of things for you two to do."

"Okay, sounds good," Kylie said. "And I like Boo's name. Very fitting for this time of year."

"Ha, thanks. I'm a sucker for Halloween, I must say. Who doesn't like an excuse to dress up and act like a kid?"

"Well, that's good to hear," Logan said, "because we actually were just talking about the upcoming Halloween dance at school and—"

"Ah, the Halloween dance. I remember those days," Miranda reminisced as she looked up toward the ceiling.

"Yes, well," Kylie said, "we were wondering if you had any good ideas for a couples costume."

"Aha. I see. A *couples* costume," Miranda said slowly. "This is a costume for you two together, I presume?"

The pair nodded.

"I see, I see. How exciting. Well, you've asked the right person, for sure. I have loads of fun Halloween costume ideas. Do you want scary, cute, fun, modern, historic, literary?"

Logan looked to Kylie who smiled and shrugged. "Fun, maybe?" Logan asked. "Cute?"

"Okay, okay. Well, how about peanut butter and jelly? Salt and pepper? I guess those wouldn't necessarily fall into the 'cute' category," Miranda said. "It's getting close to dinner time, so my mind went to food. Ben is whipping us up a nice dinner as we speak. It's great being married to a former chef. Anyway, how about something dog-related for a costume maybe? Maybe Clifford and his owner?"

Logan and Kylie looked at each other skeptically and tried not to laugh.

"Okay, um, cookies and milk? Ketchup and mustard? Is that too elementary?"

Logan quietly chuckled upon hearing Miranda go back to food choices.

"Those are cute ideas," Kylie encouraged.

"How about Wizard of Oz characters? Dorothy and Toto maybe?"

"Oh, I like that idea," Kylie said as she clutched her hands together in excitement.

"Yeah?" Logan asked. "Sounds like we have a winner then. Thanks, Miranda."

CLOVER

I wasn't home alone long before Mom and Dad arrived. They came in the door at the same time, which surprised me, but I was also super excited to see it happen. I'd been sprawled out on my bed in the living room, relaxing after my walk around town with Logan and Kylie.

Both Mom and Dad greeted me kindly and with enthusiasm. This had been the best evening I'd had in a while. First a walk with Kylie and Logan, and now a happy Mom and Dad home at the same time? I was feeling like the luckiest dog in the world. I sat down, still wagging my tail, as Mom walked into the kitchen while Dad continued petting me.

"I'm sorry, girl," Dad whispered in my ear. "I shouldn't have tried giving you up. I know now that your place is here with us at home."

I wasn't used to hearing this somber tone from Dad. I knew he wasn't talking to Mom because she was in another room. His words were just for me.

"I hope you can forgive me, Clover," Dad said as he continued petting me with his face close to mine.

I nudged him under his chin to see if I could cheer him up. I knew better than to lick his face. He'd told me "no" on every occasion I'd tried in the past, and I didn't want to anger him, especially since he was already sad.

We sat there together for a couple more minutes. It was easily the most one-on-one time I'd spent with Dad. He sat up a bit straighter before he left me, and his mouth didn't appear to be as droopy. Sometimes I loved being a dog. I'd watched as people tried to cheer up other people, but it didn't always work. I was fortunate to be able to just sit, listen, and be present to help people sometimes, and I loved to do just that.

"Clover!" Mom called out gently from the kitchen. "Ready for dinner, girl?"

There was no mistaking that she'd just said one of my favorite words. I darted to the kitchen, ready to chow down.

Dinner tasted the best it had in a while that evening. I wasn't sure if the food had changed or if it was something else that made the kibble more scrumptious that night, but I was into it.

Mom and Dad hung out in the living room for most of the evening waiting for Kylie and Vicky to come home. I was content lying down between their feet, resting the tip of my nose against one of Dad's feet and draping my tail in front of where Mom sat with her feet up on the couch.

When Vicky came home later, I'd hoped it was Kylie, but I was still happy to see her. I sat back down between Mom and Dad and waited for Kylie, hoping she'd be home soon and wondering if Logan would still be with her.

LOGAN

"Hi there, Boo," Logan said as he knelt down in front of the new chihuahua's kennel door.

"Aw, he's so cute," Kylie said as she stuck her fingers through the openings in Boo's door.

"He is awfully cute for a chihuahua," Logan said.

Kylie laughed.

"What do you mean by that, exactly?"

"Oh, I, uh," Logan said as he fumbled to find the right words, realizing that what he said might've seemed disrespectful.

"I'm just kidding," Kylie said before Logan could continue. "I know not everyone loves chihuahuas. Or little dogs in general, for that matter. He sure is a cute one, though."

"Yeah, I didn't mean to be rude. I guess I'm just more of a big dog guy?"

"You sound a little unsure," Kylie teased.

"Well, honestly, I wasn't even much of a *dog* person at all until recently. I mean, I always liked them, but just hadn't spent much time with any."

"Oh wow, right. I forget this is all new to you, too. Clover really changed things for us, huh?"

"I think so. It's funny how things turn out."

"It is. And are you… *happy* with how things have turned out?" Kylie asked as the couple continued giving Boo attention through the door.

"I can confidently say that I am," Logan said with a relaxed smile while looking directly into Kylie's eyes, happy with how bold he felt he was being.

Logan's hand reached for Kylie's, and he wondered if this would be the right opportunity for their first kiss, and his first kiss ever, but the couple jolted upright as they heard someone slamming a container down on the counter near Clover's old kennel.

"I, uh, guess we should go see what that was all about," Kylie said.

"Yes," Logan said in agreement while trying to hide his disappointment.

It was probably for the best that their first kiss didn't happen while they were crouched down in front of a chihuahua, Logan tried to rationalize to himself.

"Zoe, hey," said Logan as they approached her standing in front of a heaping pile of hollow rubber dog toys, ready to be filled with food and treats for the dogs.

"Oh, hey. I see the lovebirds have decided to help out this evening?"

Logan felt his face grow warm almost instantly and he didn't feel like he had the ability to restore it to a lighter shade any time soon. He stayed quiet and hoped Kylie would respond to Zoe's jab at them.

"We sure are," Kylie replied with a grin and self-assured tone.

Logan thought that would perturb Zoe for sure. He stayed quiet.

"Well, good," Zoe said. "None of the dogs have been out yet tonight if you want to start making the rounds. You know the drill. Take them on a quick walk or play with them depending on their temperament and make sure they take care of everything they need to before they come back inside for the night."

"Yes, we're on it," Logan said, regaining his voice, then taking a deep breath.

"Yes, we'll make sure they're all taken care of. Let us know if you need any help with the treats," Kylie said to Zoe.

Logan wasn't sure if Kylie was trying to take a kill-her-with-kindness approach to Zoe or if she was truly just being nice, but he smiled at her regardless.

"So, want to divide and conquer or should we handle this together?" Kylie asked Logan as they walked to the back of the room in order to start at the end and work their way to the front.

"I think together would be the way to go, right?"

"I was hoping you'd say that," Kylie said as she grinned and spun around before opening the last dog's kennel door.

Logan was just happy to be around Kylie. He didn't care if he was volunteering at the rescue, picking up trash, or doing absolutely nothing. While he knew he'd been nervous a fair amount, another part of him felt so calm in her presence. He welcomed this new feeling while craving more of it.

When Kylie and Logan got to the last dog, Boo, their conversation turned back to their costumes for the dance.

"So, you're on board with being Toto?" Kylie asked as they walked on the lit path outside with Boo.

"Yeah, I don't see why not," Logan replied.

"I have to say, it takes a real man to be okay with dressing up as a small dog for Halloween," Kylie said jokingly.

"Ha, well I'll try to take that as a compliment," Logan replied.

"In reality, Toto is going to end up being bigger than Dorothy, but I'm sure we can make it work. Let's keep our costume details a surprise until we see each other on the night of the dance."

"Okay, that sounds good," Logan replied, agreeing not just to please Kylie, but also because he was sure his costume creation would end up being a last-minute project for him. But he figured it couldn't be that hard to transform himself into a dog for a Halloween dance.

"Great. I'm excited to make our debut as a couple," Kylie stated.

"Oh. That's what we'll be doing?" Logan asked innocently.

"Well, I figured it would be the first time that most of the school will see us together. And it will be obvious that we're there together, whether people see us walk in as a couple or not."

"Right. I guess I hadn't thought about that part much. But I'm excited about that, too, then."

"You're funny," Kylie said.

"What?"

"You really didn't think about the other people and the fact that they'll see us there as a couple?" Kylie asked.

"No, not really. I guess… I think I was just mainly thinking about you."

"Ah," Kylie replied softly.

It was getting dark outside, so it was hard for Logan to see if Kylie's face had turned red like his had so many times before, but judging from the quiet tone of her voice, he figured it might have. He hadn't heard a reaction like that from her before.

"That's really sweet, Logan," Kylie continued.

Logan slyly bumped his hand against Kylie's as they walked until she interlocked her fingers with his. Logan suddenly couldn't even tell it was cold out any longer as he held onto Kylie's soft hand.

After Kylie and Logan dropped Boo back off in his kennel and said goodbye to Zoe and Tim, Kylie drove Logan back to the school parking lot to get his car, both in a blissful daze as they continued to hold hands.

CLOVER

I woke up to the sound of Kylie's name as I stayed lying at the base of the couch between Mom and Dad. I was ready to go upstairs and lie in Kylie's bed, but I wanted to be by the door and able to greet her when she came home.

"I can't believe she's not home yet," Dad said.

"Calm down," Mom replied. "It's only ten after 8:00. She's barely late at this point. Plus… most sixteen-year-olds would've already been given an extension to their curfew by now, you know."

"I don't care if it's ten minutes past her curfew or ten hours," Dad said in a raised voice. "Late is late. She's always home on time."

"Right, she always has been," Mom replied, "which is exactly why we should cut her some slack. If she's not home in a few minutes, let's call her." Mom's voice was starting to grow more intense. "She went to volunteer at the rescue. I'm not sure how upset we can really be here, Roy."

"I bet she's out with that Greenfield boy. Is that what she's really up to?" Dad stood up from the couch and huffed.

"I'm sure they were volunteering together, but she's a smart girl, and he seems like a really nice boy. Everything's fine. They're two teenagers spending their Friday night volunteering. Just so you know, that's kind of unheard of."

"That's what we're led to believe, at least," Dad replied, starting to pace back and forth. "What was the name of the woman at the rescue again?"

"Miranda?"

"Yeah, Miranda. Maybe I'll give her a call. Confirm their whereabouts."

"Roy, really. Just sit down. I think your job is really getting the best of you. There isn't any need to get worked up about this."

"Let's not bring my job into this."

I stayed still, hoping my name wouldn't become part of this tense conversation.

I must have fallen back to sleep because the next thing I knew, the noise of the door opening woke me up. It was Kylie! I ran to her as the back half of my body wiggled uncontrollably with excitement.

Do you want to go upstairs, Kylie? I'm ready to go upstairs. Is Logan here, too? What are we going to do next?

"Kylie," Dad said.

The deep tone of his voice made my tail sink low.

"It's fifteen minutes after 8:00."

"Oh no, is it?" Kylie said while petting me.

She didn't seem as affected by the tone of his voice and remained smiling.

"Did you not know you were late?" Mom asked Kylie.

"No, I really didn't. I'm sorry. It must've taken longer than I'd planned to drop Logan back off at school."

Kylie's eyes remained on me as she responded to Mom and Dad.

"School, huh?" Dad said. "What were you doing at school this late? I thought you were volunteering."

Kylie had a lot of words being directed at her. I looked at her, then up the stairs, then back at her, and back up the stairs again. We could probably put an end to the interrogation if we just went to her room.

"We did," Kylie said. "We were. But I'd driven us both here to walk Clover, then we went to the rescue, so I had to bring Logan back to school afterwards to get his car."

"You brought the Greenfield boy here?"

"Roy," Mom interjected.

"What?" Dad said in a challenging tone while looking at Mom with narrowed eyes.

"He didn't even come inside," Kylie replied. "I don't know what's going on right now, but I'm barely late. We were volunteering, and now I'm home."

"There will have to be a consequence for you being late, Kylie," Mom said kindly.

"Okay, what do you want me to do? Dishes?" Kylie asked casually.

I watched as she glanced toward the kitchen. Was she going to get a snack?

"It looks like the dishes are already done," Kylie said, "but I can get up early and feed Clover for the next couple of weeks or something."

"Sure," Dad said with pursed lips and a shrug. "And you're also grounded for a week." He paused. "No, you know what? Make that two weeks."

"*What?*" Kylie said in disbelief.

I sat down. The angry tones had spread and were in Kylie's voice now, too.

"You can still volunteer and obviously go to school, but if there's anything you were planning on doing outside of those two activities, well, you can cancel. Those will be the only things allowed."

"I can't believe this," Kylie said. "The Halloween dance is next week."

"Well, it doesn't look like that's the case for you," Dad replied. "You're lucky you can still volunteer."

"This is crazy. I was barely late!" Kylie exclaimed.

"It's only two weeks," Mom said quietly. "It could be worse."

"Not really," Kylie replied, not taking any queues from Mom's more subdued voice. "But, actually," Kylie continued, "the dance is at school. And you said I can still go to school. So I guess it won't actually be an issue."

"School is for school," Dad retorted. "Not dancing. At least while you're grounded. You can go to the next dance. Assuming you're not grounded again." Dad huffed.

"I really can't believe this. I've never even been late."

"Well," Dad said, "this should teach you not to be late again."

Kylie rolled her eyes and didn't reply. She went into the kitchen and grabbed some things out of the fridge before heading upstairs.

"No eating in your room, Kylie," Mom said.

Kylie continued to her room and I followed behind her. Once the door was shut, she sat down on her bed, put her head in her hands, and cried. I snuggled up to her and licked her salty wet hands.

"Oh, Clover," Kylie said as she cracked a sad smile, "you're such a good girl." She sighed. "What am I going to do now?"

I laid my head in Kylie's lap and she stroked the top of my head. After a few minutes, she ate what she'd retrieved from the fridge and shared a few bites with me.

When we finished eating, I heard Logan's voice come through Kylie's phone.

LOGAN

"Hey! Long time no talk," Logan said as he answered his phone.

"Hey," Kylie said with a sullen voice and a slight sniffle.

"Are… you okay?" Logan asked, notably concerned.

"I, um, was just grounded."

"Oh no, what? Why?"

"For being late."

"Ah, I'm so sorry if I made you late."

"Oh, no, it's far from your fault. I was the one that wanted to drive, anyway."

"How late were you? It couldn't have been that bad, right?"

"I was home fifteen minutes after curfew, so 8:15."

"Ah."

"Yeah. And I've never been late."

"I see. That's probably the problem right there. They're not used to any of their rules being bent, I guess."

"Yeah, I guess you can say that. You're lucky. You probably don't have a curfew."

"That's true. I don't. But I guess another way to look at it is you're lucky that your parents care enough to give you one."

"Right."

Kylie sighed.

"So, what does grounded mean for you?" Logan asked.

"Well, I can still go to school, obviously. And I can volunteer."

"Oh, good!"

"But… I can't do anything else."

"Oh."

"For two weeks."

"Oh," Logan repeated, with more of a sound of despair.

His heart sank. His first school dance with a girl. It was going to be their couple's debut, as Kylie had put it. He had truly been looking forward to it. The dressing up as Toto part? Not so much, but he was willing to do it for Kylie.

"Yeah, I'm so sorry. And I'm so bummed. I can't believe it. My parents just don't get it. My Dad said something stupid like 'oh, there'll be other dances,' or whatever, but I don't care about those. This was going to be our first dance, and it's the first dance of the school year and… I just really wanted to go."

"I know. I'm so sorry. Do you think they could change their minds?"

"No. I mean, if it were up to my mom, maybe. She's more lenient, but still pretty stringent. My dad? Nope. Never."

"I see. Well, it'll be okay. It's definitely disappointing, but at least you're not grounded for *life* or anything like that, I guess."

"Ha, yeah, can you imagine? Get a job? Nope. College? Nope. Actually, I guess I could still go to college since it would be considered school. I'd just volunteer and go to school forever. I can't even imagine if they took my college dreams away."

"So, just two weeks. We can make it."

"I appreciate your confidence. But I'm sorry again for you, too. I know you were looking forward to the dance."

"Well, I'll still go as Toto. Maybe I'll ask Drew if he wants to dress up as the Tin Man or something."

Logan was met by silence on the other end of the call.

"I'm just kidding," Logan said.

"Ah, ha. Sorry, I guess I can't pick up on sarcasm at this point. I'm pretty wiped."

"I bet. Well, I'm sorry you're grounded. I'm glad you'll still be able to volunteer, though. I had a really fun time with you tonight."

"Same. I always have a good time with you."

Logan smiled and started to wonder if he'd been smiling quietly too long without saying anything.

"So, I, uh," Logan said, "guess I'll see you tomorrow?"

"Yeah, sounds good. Thanks for listening. Have a good night."

"You, too. Give Clover a scratch behind the ears for me."

"I will. Bye."

"Bye," Logan replied quietly as his voice drifted off.

He looked at his phone as the call was disconnected from Kylie's end. He gradually set his phone down and decided he had to come up with a plan to make up for the Halloween dance.

CLOVER

There was so much sadness in Kylie's room that night, but Kylie seemed to have cheered up a bit after speaking with Logan. I'd experienced that effect of Logan myself, so it didn't come as a surprise to me. I kept myself pressed against Kylie's side all night, wanting to make sure she knew I was always there.

The following morning, Kylie rushed around her room getting ready before barreling down the stairs. She didn't say much that morning, solely telling Mom and Dad something about the rescue before petting me quickly and heading out the door.

Mom fed me that morning. Mom and Dad were also not very chatty.

I decided to spend my morning lying on Kylie's bed, hoping to banish any remaining sadness that continued to linger in the room.

When the family was all home that evening, everyone continued to keep their speaking to a minimum. Vicky ran off to her room, and Kylie remained in the kitchen following a quiet dinner. She sat at the table while working on her books and papers from her bag. I stayed lying by her feet even though the floor was cold.

Kylie didn't look up at Mom when she came in and sat down next to her.

"Kylie, I want you to know that that was a hard decision we had to make last night."

"Mhmm," Kylie responded.

"I'm sorry you won't be able to go to your dance."

Kylie didn't reply.

"Can you look at me, please?" Mom asked.

Kylie looked up, put her pencil down, and sat back in her chair while crossing her arms.

"I said I'm sorry," Mom said.

"Yes, I heard that," Kylie replied.

"Okay."

"Okay."

"Were… you planning on going to the dance with Logan or was it more of a dance with friends?"

"Logan."

"I see. I'm sure that must be upsetting."

Kylie glanced down toward me and started banging her right heel against the leg of her chair. Was she about to get up? I stared at her feet. If she stood up, I was ready to follow.

"You really like him, huh?" Mom asked.

Kylie nodded her head.

"That's good. He seems really nice."

"He is."

"Good. Well, at least you both can still go to the rescue to volunteer. We're not taking *everything* away."

"No. Just the most important night for me. No big deal, right? Because you're sorry."

"Okay, look, I was trying to apologize and be understanding, but if you're going to give me attitude, then I think we're done here."

Kylie kicked the leg of the chair harder, then stopped. I eyed Mom's feet as she walked away from the table, keeping my head low to the floor over my front paws. Kylie reached down and petted my head.

Are we going to go upstairs now?

I slept soundly lying next to Kylie that night, cuddled against her side. She no longer seemed as sad, but she did seem more tense. She'd thrown her bag to her bedroom floor with a little more gusto than I was used to seeing, then shut her door louder than I'd heard her shut it before. Kylie was normally so happy. It was hard to see her like this, but I'd come to find that sometimes this happened with even the cheeriest of people. I felt sure that things would turn around again for Kylie.

LOGAN

Come Saturday afternoon, Logan knew he had to begin his job search. He got into his car, unsure of his destination. Before starting his car, he decided to call Seth.

"Hey, man," Seth answered. "It's been a bit. I'm glad you called."

"Yeah, how's it going?" Logan asked.

"Well, I'm working again."

"Oh, that's great to hear! At River Ridge Chicken again?"

"What?" Seth chuckled. "No way, man. I'm not going back to RRC. Actually, it's funny you asked because Bill did call me up the other day to ask me, actually he *told* me now that I'm thinking about it, to come back! Can you believe it? Like I would willingly go back to that place. I haven't even eaten any chicken since I was fired."

"Dude, yikes. I'm glad he offered you your job back, though. He must've known he was in the wrong."

"I guess," Seth replied.

"So where are you working then?"

"Ha, well that's a funny story too, actually. Right across the street."

"Wait, really? At McCorley's?"

Logan's mind flashed back to finding Clover right outside of Seth's new workplace.

"Yeah, man. I can't even begin to tell you what an amazing change it is over there. Everyone's treated well, our schedules aren't constantly changing, there's no drama, and, the best part, people *tip*."

"Ah, wow," Logan replied, envisioning money left on tables. It was an enticing image.

"Yeah, I swear I made more there last weekend than I typically did in a full week at RRC."

Logan was glad Seth sounded so happy.

"Plus," Seth continued, "did I mention there's no drama and there aren't any schedule issues?" he asked, ensuring the point was getting across. "It's bliss, man. Pure. Bliss. How are things in chicken land?"

"Well," Logan said before pausing. "I quit."

The words didn't come out as strong as he'd hoped. He'd wanted to sound sure and proud.

"What? I didn't know that," Seth replied, sounding sincerely concerned and surprised. Logan realized he must not have listened to the voicemail he'd left him. "When?"

"A couple days ago. I was getting pretty tired of Bill."

"Ha, yeah. Really, though, good for you. I wonder how long the others will last. Or if us leaving was a wakeup call for Bill. Or... do you think *he'll* get fired? Can he even get fired? I don't know how that works."

"Ha, yeah, me neither. I hope he's not around much longer for everyone else's sake. But I'm now in the job-hunting game. Any tips?"

"Yeah. Come work at McCorley's, man. We're looking for another server and someone to help in the kitchen. I'm sure you could get either position if you wanted. Interested?"

Logan's eyes widened in excitement.

"Of course," Logan replied. "That would be amazing," he continued, not worried about sounding too enthusiastic. He was too relieved to care.

"Okay," Seth said. "Well, I was planning on heading in for my shift right before 6:00, but the manager heads out at 5:00 today, so if I go in now, I might be able to catch her and talk you up."

Logan was beaming. He hadn't imagined such an exciting opportunity from his call to Seth. He'd mainly just wanted to check in on him to make sure he was doing okay.

"You free tonight if she decides she wants you to come in?" Seth asked.

"Yup, I'm free."

"Great. I'll let you know. Man, that would be great working together again. It's such a change from RRC and if they hired me, they'll definitely hire you."

"Ha, well thanks, Seth. I appreciate it."

"I'll give you a shout in a few. Later."

"Later."

Logan sat back in his driver's seat and let out a breath as he continued smiling. He hadn't even left his driveway and he already felt confident that he'd scored a new job.

CLOVER

Kylie spent most of the evening in her room after she came home, and I wasn't about to be upset about it. Cozying up to her in her bed was officially one of my favorite places to be. The blankets always seemed to find themselves in new and exciting layers that always molded to my body in the most comfortable way.

I'd dozed prior to hearing Kylie answer her phone. I couldn't hear who she was speaking to at first, but judging from the smile on her face, I figured it had to be Logan. Once she set her phone down, I could hear him. I stared at Kylie's phone as I listened to his voice, wishing I could smell him as he talked.

"Well, I have some exciting news," Logan said.

"Oh yeah?" Kylie asked while sitting up on her bed. "I could benefit from hearing some good news."

"I got a new job."

"What? Really? Where?"

"At McCorley's!"

"Oh wow. That place is fantastic."

"It is. I can't believe it. One of my old co-workers started working there recently and loves it."

"That's great. So wait, what happened to River Ridge Chicken? I didn't know you were considering working somewhere else."

"Well, I hadn't been, until my boss told me that I couldn't have Thursday night off."

"Oh, no."

"Yeah, I mean, it really wasn't just that. It was time to move on. And it ended up landing me at McCorley's, so all's well that ends well I'm thinking."

"I guess so! I'm happy you're excited about it. And isn't that where you found Clover?"

I moved closer to Kylie's side upon hearing my name, then rolled over and stretched out, awaiting a soothing belly rub.

"It is," Logan replied. "Maybe Clover was trying to tell me something all along, huh? I'll have to thank her next time I see her. How's she doing?"

Kylie obliged and rubbed my tummy as I heard Logan say my name.

"Oh, good," Kylie replied. "Just doing the usual, cuddled up on my bed."

"Nice. Sounds relaxing."

"It is. But it's also kind of disheartening to think about how this is pretty much all I'll be doing for two weeks."

"Well, at least you can volunteer, right?"

"Yes, thank goodness. That was my saving grace today. I actually had a really good time and plan on going again tomorrow. And everyone suggested that I bring Clover with me."

"Oh, good. That'll be fun," Logan replied.

"What about you? Do you have your new schedule for work?"

"I do. They were pretty desperate for a new server, so I actually start training tomorrow morning at 8:00, then will be working each night through Wednesday, but, then I'll have two days off. So, I was hoping we could volunteer together Thursday and Friday?"

"Oh wow, that's a busy schedule you have there. They must be so glad to have you. And I'd love to volunteer with you on Friday. My parents are having company over for dinner on Thursday apparently, and, of course, I'm expected to be here."

"Okay. Friday it is. That works great, actually, since it would've been the night of the dance."

"Ah, right. The dance. I've tried to forget about that."

The tone of Kylie's voice started to sound sad. I nudged her arm. Maybe they should talk about me again.

"We'll still have fun together," Logan said.

"I don't doubt it. We always do."

My eyes went back and forth between Kylie and her phone as each of them spoke. I was happy to see Kylie smile again. They continued to talk as I stretched out and nuzzled my nose against Kylie's leg. I must have drifted off to sleep again, because the next thing I knew, the room was dark when I opened my eyes, and I found myself having a staring contest with a stuffed animal that was sitting on top of Kylie's book-shelf. I lost, but it was a fierce competition. They probably only closed their eyes once everyone else's were closed.

LOGAN

Logan awoke early Sunday morning, eager to start his first day at McCorley's. His excitement continued as he approached River Ridge Chicken, feeling fortunate that that wasn't going to be his final destination. Before he could continue to relish in this moment of freedom, he saw Kylie's car parked outside McCorley's.

"Kylie," Logan said as he got out of his car, looking over at her and Clover, hoping everything was okay. "What's going on?"

"Oh, well, we just wanted to wish you good luck before your big day," Kylie said as Clover pulled her closer to Logan to say hello.

"Wow, well this is the best surprise," Logan replied as he bent down to greet Clover.

"I figured you'd get here early," Kylie said. "And you proved me right," she continued as she laughed while watching Clover rub up against Logan's leg, soaking in his affection.

"Yeah, I guess I was pretty excited about my first day. Had I only known I was also going to get to see you two! Aren't you worried about being grounded though?"

"No, I'll be headed out in a minute. I know you have to get going. Then Clover and I will be on our way to the rescue. But I didn't want you to start your first day without giving you this."

Logan's heartbeat quickened as he watched Kylie reach into her pocket.

"It's an old copper coin," Kylie said. "But it's not just any old coin. My grandparents gave this to me when I was a kid after their trip to Greece. They used to tell me stories about everywhere the coin had been. It's for good luck. And I want you to take it for your first day."

Logan didn't know how to respond. He couldn't believe how sweet this gesture was.

"Here," Kylie said as she placed the coin in Logan's hand. "Its adventure continues. I hope you have a great first day, Logan."

"Thank you, Kylie," he replied as he carefully placed the good luck charm in his pocket. He'd never had anyone do something so unexpected and thoughtful before.

"Of course," Kylie replied as Clover sat down and stared up expectantly. "It looks like it's time for us to get going before Clover thinks we're all going on a walk together."

The rest of Logan's morning was full of learning new processes, procedures, and people at McCorley's while thinking of Kylie and Clover during any free minute he had.

Logan went straight to his bed upon returning home and sprawled out with a heavy sigh. He was beat. But grateful.

Logan texted Kylie to say good night early, then drifted off to sleep.

CLOVER

Kylie had taken me back to Miranda's place with the dog room for the day. I didn't really want to leave her car when we arrived, but I saw Miranda outside the front door and decided I wouldn't mind saying hi to her. Kylie also wasn't acting strange, so there wasn't anything to lead me to believe that I should be worried.

I followed Kylie around as she prepared treats and took some of my old dog room friends outside. It was nice hanging out with everyone again, but I did feel bad walking around the room as a free dog while the others were stuck in their closets.

I was familiar with everyone in the dog room except one new arrival that Kylie called Boo. He was small and started shaking when I appeared in front of his closet door, so I didn't stay at his door long.

I spent some time outside with Kylie and different groups of dogs throughout the day. Miranda and Ben's dog, Kiwi, joined us for most of the day as well.

Toward the end of our time at the dog room, I did go back to visit Boo. This time, I sat down and focused my attention on the door, not looking at this new, timid dog. Eventually he came closer to his closet door. I looked over and he sat down, no longer shaking. He stood and crept a little closer, then a little more, until his nose was jutting out from his closet. I moved my nose closer to his and was happy he didn't hesitate when our noses touched.

I wondered if he was missing a family. And if he'd have to stay here long. It wasn't long ago that I was stuck like him, and I wished I could tell him that things would get better. The right person for him would come along, and in the meantime, it wasn't *all* that bad in the dog room. It'd be better if they'd had blankets or cushy floors, though.

"Aw, look at these two," Kylie said as she stood next to me and spoke to an older woman in the dog room that I wasn't familiar with.

"That's pretty cute," the older woman said. "Ever think of adopting two dogs?"

"Ha, if it were up to me, I'd have a whole house full of dogs, but right now I'm just fortunate to have Clover."

"Well, maybe someday you'll have more then," the woman said. "I'm sure Boo will find a good home eventually. I'm hoping a lot of them get adopted before the holidays. Things usually pick up in November and December."

"Oh, good," Kylie replied. "There are so many great dogs here. It's amazing what Miranda and Ben have done."

"It really is," the woman replied. "And what they say is right. Each dog really is one-of-a-kind, just like people.

I've learned a lot about dogs, and myself, during my time volunteering here."

I watched as Kylie continued to listen to the woman.

"You might be thinking I'm too old to say something like that," the woman said to Kylie, "but I'll tell you, the lessons never stop coming. As long as you're willing to continue learning."

Kylie smiled. "I like that," she replied.

The next day, Kylie spent most of the day away at what I'd started to think was called school. It was harder to see her leave after spending most of the previous day with her.

When Kylie came home, I wondered if we'd be going back to see Miranda. We ended up hanging out on her bed while she tended to some papers from her bag instead. I was happy to stay home that night and relax with Kylie.

LOGAN

Monday after school, Logan knew he had to see Miranda at the rescue before he headed to work. He had an idea for Kylie that he needed Miranda and Ben's help with. He gave the rescue a call before he drove over to make sure Miranda would be available.

"Hi, Miranda, it's Logan."

"Ah, yes. I haven't seen you in a few days. How has everything been?"

"Oh, good, thanks. I actually have a new job, so that's taken up a lot of my time lately, but I do plan on coming in Thursday to volunteer."

"Ah, that's great to hear. And congrats on your new job. I hope it's a good one."

"It is, yeah. Thank you. I'm working over at McCorley's as a server."

"Ah, that's wonderful. I love that place. Ben and I try to get there every couple of months or so. It's our go-to for good food, atmosphere, and people. Definitely a great fit for you, I'd say."

"Oh, thank you. I've really enjoyed my time there so far. So, I was actually hoping to catch up with you and run an idea by you if you're around?"

"I am, yes. Would this idea happen to involve your girlfriend, Kylie, by any chance? She is just so lovely. She spent so much time here this past weekend, and the dogs just loved it. As did we. She's a gem."

"Ha, yes, she's definitely great. No argument there. We're technically not boyfriend-girlfriend, th—"

"Oh you youngsters and your shenanigans. Well, whatever they call it these days," Miranda said.

"Ha, no, it's not like that. We just, haven't made anything official yet, you know?"

"Aha, I see. Okay, sure." Miranda chuckled. "But yes, to answer your question, I'm here. I'll be around for a couple more hours if you want to stop by."

"Great, I have about an hour before I have to head to work. I'll see you soon."

Logan went in to see Miranda and explained what he was hoping to do as a surprise for Kylie on Friday night at the rescue. Miranda and Ben were more than willing to help out. By the time Logan left, he couldn't wait for Friday to come. He wasn't looking forward to keeping his plan a secret from Kylie, but he knew it would end up being worth it.

Logan continued to stay busy with school and work throughout the week, which he appreciated since every time he seemed to have a free minute, he would think about his surprise for Kylie on Friday, and Friday always seemed so far away.

On Thursday night after volunteering at the rescue, Logan spread out his books and homework on his bed, then called Kylie.

"Hey, Kylie," Logan said with a broad grin.

He felt completely burnt out after working so much and then volunteering that evening, but it wasn't hard for him to muster up enough energy to be excited to speak with Kylie.

"How did your dinner with your parents' friends go tonight?"

"Um, well, I think that's a better question for Clover. For me, it was fine. But poor Clover was *not* happy. She wouldn't even stay in the same room as the visitors. It was actually the same couple that had come over the other night. The people that were super interested in Clover. The couple that I thought we were going to lose her to."

"Oh. Oh, no."

Logan thought back to the conversation he overheard at school after Kylie's concert.

"I know," Kylie said. "I mean, I'm so glad that that didn't end up happening, but it was almost like Clover knew that that could've happened, you know? She didn't want to say hi to them and pretty much ran and hid when they came inside."

"That's definitely strange," Logan said, trying to sound as convincing as possible while he attempted to squash the memory of her parents' post-concert conversation from his mind. "I guess I'd have a hard time trusting that couple, then. If Clover didn't like them."

"I agree. I didn't say much at dinner. It was pretty weird. But anyway, how was your time volunteering tonight?"

"Oh, good. The usual," Logan said in an effort to make it sound boring so he wouldn't be asked too many questions.

While he'd cleaned a few kennels and taken some dogs out, he'd actually spent most of his evening at the rescue working on his surprise for Kylie. Miranda and Ben had been gracious enough to help Logan out and promised to finish the final details before the following evening. Logan was grateful for their willingness to complete the setup for the surprise so that he'd have enough time to finish his homework that night.

"How's Boo doing?" Kylie asked.

"Good," Logan replied. "He seems to be settling in a bit more. He even played with a couple of the other smaller dogs while they were outside tonight."

"Aw, that's great. He had the cutest moment with Clover over the weekend. Boo had stuck his nose out of his kennel door, and they ended up pretty much nose kissing. I couldn't believe it. It was so cute."

"I'm glad they're getting along. I'm looking forward to tomorrow," Logan said as he flipped through the pages of his notebook from its worn corner.

"Same here. I've been looking forward to Friday night all week."

Logan could hear the smile in Kylie's voice.

"Well, if we're being honest, so have I," Logan said.

"Aw," Kylie replied. "I'm thinking I'll bring Clover again tomorrow night, too."

"That'd be great. I'd love to see her again."

"Well, I'm sure she'll be ecstatic to see you, too. Even though she lives with me, I think you'll forever be her number one."

"Ha, I think she loves you just as much."

"Hmmm… maybe," Kylie said as she chuckled. "Time for me to get some shut eye. See you tomorrow, Logan."

"Yes, see you tomorrow, Kylie," Logan replied.

Logan was beaming when he got off the phone. He loved talking to Kylie. And now that Friday was finally about to arrive, Logan felt like a kid the night before Christmas. Even without the school dance, he knew Friday night would still be a major moment for their relationship.

CLOVER

Hearing Logan's voice come through Kylie's phone had been the best part of my day. The events that had happened at home prior to Logan calling were unexpected, and slightly traumatic.

My dognappers had visited.

They had come inside.

And they ate food with my family.

No one stopped them. No one asked them to leave. No one seemed alarmed, but me.

I hid right away. I wasn't going anywhere with them again even if they did plan on saying the word "walk." The whole family was around this time, so I figured I'd have backup this time if I needed it, but I wasn't willing to get too close and leave things up to chance. I was determined to keep my distance and stay as safe as possible.

The hospitality I witnessed from Kylie's family to the dognappers made me wonder if the family was really good at acting or if they were unaware of how I'd had to escape from these people not that long ago. They must not have known that the couple had taken me and trapped me, leaving me to find my own way back home. What if they tried to take them next?

I didn't get any scraps from the dinner table that night. I was typically able to gather up some crumbs or sneak a bit of food from Kylie or Vicky's hand, but I didn't approach the table.

When the dognappers left, I was relieved that Kylie wanted to retreat to her room where it was safe. I still hadn't recovered from seeing the unwelcomed visitors, but my muscles started to relax after coming upstairs, and they returned close to their normal state as Kylie spoke with Logan. I hoped I'd be seeing him again soon.

LOGAN

"Hey, wait up!" Logan heard someone call to him as he walked into school.

He hoped it was Kylie and was happy to see that it was as he turned around.

"Hey! I wasn't expecting to see you so early this morning," Logan said to Kylie as she caught up with him.

"I know. I found myself up early, probably excited for tonight."

"I see. And what's happening tonight?" Logan said, feigning ignorance before cracking a smile.

"Well, aren't you a joker this morning," Kylie replied with a grin. "So, what's the plan for tonight? Do you want to just meet at the rescue?"

"Sure, that sounds good. I was planning on getting there around 4:00," Logan said.

"Perfect. That'll give me enough time to go home and get Clover before heading out."

Kylie paused.

"And, in the meantime," she continued, "I guess we'll just do our best to ignore all talk about the dance today."

"Right," Logan said. "Wait, is there even a dance tonight?"

"Aha, the jokes continue from Mr. Funny Man. Did you have coffee this morning or something?"

"I think it's just adrenaline. Hoping I don't crash later," Logan replied, equally hoping that his self-assured tone would last the entire day as he opened the front door for Kylie.

"I'm sure you'll be fine," Kylie said while nudging her elbow against Logan's arm as they walked into the building together.

"Yeah, I'm sure we'll make it through today unscathed and see each other at the rescue in no time."

Logan figured if he said it aloud, maybe it would have more of a chance of coming true.

"Yes, sounds like a plan. Catch you later," Kylie said with a grin as she headed off to her locker.

Logan started running through his mental to-do list for the evening as he spun the dial on his locker.

"Hey, man, it's been a while," Drew said as Logan opened his locker door.

"Yeah, hey. What's up?" Logan asked as he started rummaging through papers and books.

"Oh, well, you know, probably the same thing as you, right?" Drew asked. "Just thinking about the big Halloween dance tonight."

"Right, I guess I haven't had a chance to tell you, but I won't be going," Logan replied while still focused on getting his belongings together.

"What? I thought for sure you were going to be going with Kylie."

"Yeah, well, I was," Logan said as he shut his locker door. "We were. But… change of plans."

"What? Really?"

"Yeah, it's kind of a long story, but we'll still be hanging out later while we're volunteering at the rescue."

"Wow, man. You guys are like the picture-perfect couple for college applications. Skipping a dance to volunteer? Man," Drew said.

Logan leaned against his locker and decided to ignore any condescension in Drew's voice.

"Ha, yeah, I guess so. But it sounds like you'll be going to the dance after all?"

"Yeah man, I asked Sierra Myers. It was a long shot, I know. Turns out she and her boyfriend broke up not that long ago, and I don't think anyone else had the guts to ask her, so anyway, she said yes."

"Wow, that's great. You seem excited."

"Man, I am. I haven't been this excited about a school dance… maybe ever."

"Ha, that's good to hear. I'm sorry I won't be there to witness it."

Even though Drew had had his weird moments when it came to Logan spending time with Kylie, Logan was still happy for him.

"Yeah, sorry for you guys, too, even though it sounds like you'll be just as content."

"Yeah, actually, I have a favor to ask you. You're still part of the student council group that plans these dances, right?"

"I mean, technically, yes, but really, I'm not doing much of anything. How come?"

"Would you be able to get me a copy of the playlist for tonight's dance?"

"Oh, sure, not a problem. I'll get it from Greg and can give it to you before science class later."

"Great, appreciate it."

Logan wondered if Drew was going to ask why he wanted it, but luckily the bell rang, and he said a quick good-bye before heading off to his first class of the day, hoping it would fly by along with the rest of them.

CLOVER

Kylie had gone off to school, earlier than usual, leaving me to peruse the house on my own for the day. After checking all the rooms to see if anything interesting was left out or behind, I took a nap in Mom and Dad's closet. The floor was extra soft where I had once thrown up. After my nap, I moved on to staring at the critters that ran around in the backyard. They only did this while I was inside.

Fortunately, Kylie was the first one home. She entered the house humming a sweet tune before elegantly tossing her jacket on the coat rack. She even spun around as she made herself a snack and fed me my dinner. I was thrilled to see Kylie like this. I hadn't seen her this happy at home before.

After we ate dinner, I helped Kylie try on clothes in her room. Each time she took an outfit off and threw it on the floor, I'd pick up the garments and place them at her feet. She laughed and petted me each time. Afterwards, I watched Kylie as she smudged things on her face in the bathroom while looking at her reflection. She was still cheery and humming, so I followed her expectantly from room to room smiling, trotting, and ready to see what would happen next.

When she grabbed my leash, I thought we were going to go for a walk, but I was pleasantly surprised that Kylie wanted me to jump into the backseat of her car instead.

Were we going to meet up with Logan?

I was growing fairly certain that her jovial demeanor meant we'd be seeing him. Whenever Kylie was this happy, he usually played a role.

We arrived at Miranda's place, and Kylie retrieved me from the backseat. Kylie always looked pretty, but she was extra striking this evening. I wondered if whatever she'd smudged on her face earlier was involved in creating her enhanced look.

I whimpered and tugged at my leash upon seeing Logan at the front door of the building, waiting for us.

"Go on, Clover," Kylie said to me as she dropped my leash.

I barreled toward Logan. After our standard session of cuddles and greetings, I noticed there was something different about him tonight, too. His hair seemed to be neater, and he smelled different. Less like food and more like soap, but in a better way than the soapy scent of the dognappers. I'd smelled Logan like this before, but it usually wasn't this strong. Personally, I missed the chicken scent.

LOGAN

Logan stood and brushed his pants off after petting Clover. His eyes met Kylie's as she walked toward him.

"Kylie, you look…" Logan paused. "I'm not even sure I have the right word."

"Well, hopefully you're searching for a good one," Kylie joked, easing some tension as she glanced toward the ground.

"Of course. You look beautiful, but that word doesn't do you justice. Radiant, maybe. You look radiant," Logan said in a trance.

Kylie grinned and picked up Clover's leash. Clover sat down between Logan and Kylie as they continued speaking.

"Well, thank you," Kylie replied with a slight curtsy. "I know we're just volunteering, but I still wanted to get a little dressed up, considering we would've been at the dance tonight."

"Ah, yes, the dance," Logan replied, as if he could've forgotten. "I'm sorry we couldn't make it there tonight, but I'm glad we still get to spend the evening together."

Logan had moved on from any initial disappointment that he'd had about not being able to attend the dance with

Kylie since he'd started planning his surprise for her. He felt that the night could end up being even more special at the rescue with Kylie.

"Same," Kylie said with a grin as they walked inside to see Ben dressed in a suit and tie.

"Good evening," said Ben. "Right this way, you two."

"Hey, Ben," Kylie said. "What's, uh, going on here?" Kylie asked speculatively while flashing a side glance over to Logan.

Logan grinned and gave Ben a nod to continue.

"Ah, no questions, my dear," said Ben. "You'll see, you'll see."

Ben led Kylie and Logan into the rescue's function room, where they'd first sat together as new volunteers.

The room was decked out in twinkling white holiday lights, truly transforming the room from its standard mundane appearance to a romantic oasis. Logan figured it had to look even better than the transformed school gym did for the Halloween dance. There was a small strobe light flashing against one of the walls that spread a rainbow of changing colors throughout the room and a table for two in the center that had a lit lantern and two place settings.

Logan beamed as he took in Kylie's reaction to the surprise. Her mouth was agape as she scanned the room.

"Is this for us?" Kylie asked in awe.

"Yes, I wanted to surprise you," Logan said as he took Kylie's hand. "I felt terrible when I found out we weren't going to be able to make it to the dance. I know how much you'd been looking forward to it and frankly, I was too. So I wanted to do something special for you. For us. We can still make our relationship debut tonight. It will just look a little different than we'd expected."

"Wow, Logan. I truly can't believe this," Kylie replied as she squeezed Logan's hand and continued looking around. "This is beautiful. Amazing. Now I'm the one with the lack of the right words to describe what I'm seeing," Kylie said with a laugh.

"I'm glad you like it," Logan said as they looked at each other and smiled.

"Sorry to interrupt the moment, you two," Ben interjected, "but, we have dinner that will be ready to be served in just a few minutes if you want to both take a seat at your table."

"Wow, this is all so elegant and sophisticated," Kylie replied to Ben. "I definitely feel underdressed now."

"Well, luckily for you both," Ben said, "there is no true dress code for the evening, and there also isn't anyone around to judge," he continued as he shrugged. "I'll be back with some drinks in just a moment."

"I still can't believe this," Kylie said as they sat down at the table. "So you've been planning this the whole time?"

"Well, since Monday, yes. Miranda and Ben have been so helpful as you can see. We worked on decorating the room last night."

Logan picked up his napkin and almost put it in his lap before realizing he should probably wait for the food to arrive.

"Wow," Kylie replied, still in awe. "Hands down, this is the nicest thing anyone has ever done for me."

"I'm happy we'll still be able to have a fun night together," Logan said as he tried to sneak his napkin back in place on the table.

"Me too," Kylie said as she reached out to hold Logan's hand.

Ben arrived with two sparkling waters in champagne flutes.

"Here are your non-alcoholic beverages for the evening," Ben said as he placed the drinks down on the table. "And I'll be back shortly with the main course."

"Thank you, Ben," Logan said before taking a sip of water.

"Yes, thank you," said Kylie, her eyes focused on Logan.

CLOVER

I was in a new room at Miranda's place, and since entering, it seemed like Kylie and Logan had forgotten I even existed. I'd seen this behavior from them before, and I was inclined to let it go, considering how happy they seemed. I stayed between them lying down on the floor as they sat at a table and were catered to by Ben. It was a surprising situation. I'd fully expected that we'd be making the typical rounds in and out of the dog room when we'd arrived, but I was always down for something new, especially when both Kylie and Logan were involved.

I listened to them talk as they ate their dinner together. Kylie dropped me a scrap from time to time, which had become a sort of ritual of ours. One of my favorites, I had to say. The food that they were eating was indisputably scrumptious, and from what I could tell, Logan and Kylie thought the same. It was nice seeing them together sharing a meal. It seemed like something that people often did when they loved each other.

After they finished their dinner, Ben appeared and mentioned the word "dessert," which made both Kylie and Logan laugh.

"I'm not sure I could eat another bite," Kylie said.

"Same," said Logan. "But this meal was probably the best food I've ever eaten. You really made all of this?"

"Oh, yes, yes," Ben replied as he took the couple's dishes. "Stir fry is one of our specialties."

"I would have to agree," said Kylie.

"I'm glad to hear you both enjoyed your meals. I'll bring dessert out, but no pressure on eating it. It will be there if you're interested in it later," Ben said.

"That sounds good, thank you," Logan said.

As Ben walked away, music started to play, and the lights dimmed more.

"Oh, no way," Kylie said.

"Would you like to dance?" Logan asked as he stood and extended his hand to Kylie.

"Oh my gosh, I love this song," Kylie said enthusiastically as she put her hand in Logan's and stood. "Is this the radio?"

"I was actually able to get the playlist for tonight's dance. I thought we could have our own here."

"Wow, Logan. That's so sweet. And yes, I would love to dance."

I stood up as Kylie and Logan left the table and started dancing. Kylie spun around and laughed, while Logan moved slightly from side to side with his feet planted. I hadn't seen too many people dance in my life, but I'd never seen someone dance quite like Logan before, either. Regardless, they both continued to be in their blissful bubble. I did join them off and on while they danced, though, just to make sure they knew I was still there.

Ben came back after a few songs to set some more food down on the table. I wondered if it would taste as good as the scraps from dinner. He also brought Kiwi with him. I was so excited to see her. We ran around the perimeter of the room before settling down. We'd check on Logan and Kylie from time to time between relaxing and playing.

The music slowed as I sat down next to Kiwi. I watched the couple as they hesitantly placed their arms around each other and started to sway from side to side in unison. It was almost as if Logan had convinced Kylie to adapt to his style of dancing, although the movements did appear to be more appropriate for the low-key tune that was now playing.

A variety of melodies and movements continued throughout the evening before ending with another slow song.

Logan and Kylie embraced again during the last song with more ease and grace. I couldn't hear what they were mumbling to each other, but joy continued to radiate from them both. Kiwi and I continued to lie down and watch quietly. That is, until I saw their faces move in closer to each other. I sat up. Was Kylie trying to figure out what Logan smelled like? Was Logan getting a closer look at her face smudges?

Then the most unexpected thing happened.

Their lips touched briefly. Then again. I wasn't sure if they were licking each other or accidentally bumping faces while sniffing each other. It was an odd thing to view. I barked.

"Clover, it's okay," Kylie said as she laughed. "It's called a kiss."

A kiss. A kiss? I wasn't sure about this. I walked over to them, leaving Kiwi lying on the floor. She was clearly less surprised about the odd display Kylie and Logan had just put on than I was.

LOGAN

"Do you think she's ever seen people kiss before?" Logan asked.

"I don't know. I mean, I would think she would've seen my parents kiss by now… but, maybe not with everything that's been going on lately. They've seemed pretty stressed out."

Kylie looked down at Clover. "Was this the first kiss you've ever witnessed, girl?"

Clover sat down.

"I'll take that as a yes," Kylie said with a giggle. "And hopefully it won't be the last," she said as she turned back to Logan with a wide smile on her face. "I would say this turned out to be the most unexpectedly perfect couple's debut."

Logan smiled back at Kylie as the song finished and they stopped dancing.

"I would wholeheartedly agree with that," Logan replied.

"So, now for some dessert after all of that dancing?" Kylie asked.

"That sounds perfect," Logan said as they walked back to the table hand in hand.

"Oh, no," Kylie said as she looked at the table.

Logan glanced at the cleared tabletop before his eyes met two small plates on the floor with a distinct sheen that he knew could've only resulted from a dog's work.

"Clover," Logan said in a low voice. "Kiwi? Did you two do this?"

"Oh my, look at their faces," Kylie said as she laughed. "The white markings on Clover's face must've hidden the frosting pretty well before, but I can see it now. And look at Kiwi. It's pretty hard to hide white frosting when you're a black lab, huh, girl?" Kylie said as she looked over at Kiwi.

Both Clover and Kiwi wagged their tails.

"I guess we can't really be mad at them," Logan said. "We pretty much left the cake there for their taking."

"Yeah, I guess you're right," Kylie replied. "I honestly forgot they were even in here for most of the night. I think I was pretty caught up in our dancing."

"Same. No regrets here," Logan replied.

They both laughed.

"Hey, what time is it?" Kylie asked.

Logan took his phone out of his pocket.

"It is… 7:48. Will you be able to make it home on time?"

"Yes," Kylie said as she grabbed her purse. "If I leave right now. Thank you *so* much for this incredible night, Logan. I know I'll never forget it."

"Thank *you*," Logan replied, wondering if they were always supposed to kiss when they left each other from here on out.

Kylie was too focused on getting home, though, so he figured that probably wouldn't be the case. Logan clipped Clover's leash to her harness and handed it to Kylie. Kylie said a quick goodbye while grabbing her jacket, then ran out the door.

Logan bent down to wipe the frosting off Kiwi's face as Ben walked back into the room with Miranda.

"We just saw Kylie run out. Is everything okay?"

"Oh, yeah," Logan replied. "More than okay. She just had to get back home before her curfew. But tonight was amazing. Thank you, both. I couldn't have done this without you two."

"Oh, you know we're happy to help," Miranda replied. "I'm glad we were able to contribute to this for you two. It sounds like you had a good time."

"We did, thank you."

"And," Ben said as he looked at the empty dessert plates that sat on the table, "it looks like you both ended up having room for dessert after all?"

"Uh, yes," Logan said as he shot Kiwi a quick glance. "I guess we did."

"Well, I'm sure you have to run home too, so don't worry about cleaning up. We'll take care of it," Miranda said.

"Are you sure?" Logan asked.

"Yes, it's not a problem," she replied. "And I actually like the lights in here. Maybe we'll keep them up for the holidays."

"I love that idea," Ben said. "This place needs more of that holiday spirit."

"Well, thank you both again," Logan said as he grabbed his coat. "I'll see you soon."

Logan was nearly skipping as he made his way to his car, unable to wipe the smile from his face even if he wanted to.

He glanced down at his phone when he got into his car and saw a few text messages. One was from Drew.

Hope your surprise went well with Kylie. Wanted to let you know that Sierra and I made our couple's debut tonight. She's amazing. Catch up with you soon.

Logan grinned. He was happy Drew found someone he clicked with.

The next message he saw was from Kylie.

Made it home with two minutes to spare, so all went well. No questions asked. Thank you for such a surprising and special night.

Logan responded to both messages, then sat back in his car and let out a deep breath. He felt like things were really falling into place for him.

CLOVER

A few days after I'd seen Logan in the room with all of the lights and music at Miranda's, Kylie and I met up with him again at what Kylie referred to as Logan's work.

"Hey!" Logan shouted to us from across the street.

"Hey!" Kylie shouted back.

I stood and wagged my tail, ready for his greeting.

"What were you doing over at River Ridge Chicken? When you said you had a few minutes to spare before work, I thought you were talking about McCorley's."

"Oh, yes, no, nothing's changed," Logan said as he approached me and Kylie. "I just had to run in and get my last paycheck from RRC," he explained as he reached down to scratch behind my ears.

"Ah, I see. That must've been exciting then. Your last time going in there!" Kylie exclaimed as she looked at him with expectant eyes.

I was sure I had a similar expression on my own face. I was waiting for Logan to squat down so I could provide a proper greeting. He must've noticed because the next thing I knew, I was able to squish my face against his.

"Hey there, Clover," Logan said to me as he chuckled. "It's good to see you too, girl."

Much to my surprise, Logan was completely covered in his amazing chicken scent. I sniffed and whined in delight. This intoxicatingly blissful smell hadn't been this strong since the first day I'd met him. He continued to pet me, so I rubbed up against him, hoping some of the glorious aromas would transfer to my fur so I could smell them again later.

"Man, she just gives you more and more affection each time she sees you, huh?" Kylie asked with a laugh.

"You're a good girl, Clover," Logan said to me.

I wagged my tail. I loved when he said that. His voice was always so sincere and full of love when he said my name and told me I was good.

Logan stood up and started talking softly with Kylie. I watched intently, curious if their faces would rub together again and unsure about how I'd react if they did.

After a couple of minutes, it didn't seem like that was going to happen. They were clearly lost in each other as usual, so I slipped out of Kylie's grasp and ran over to the alley. That alley had one of the best trash containers I'd ever eaten out of. I tipped it over and started scarfing down a variety of flavorful pieces of food. It was even better than I'd anticipated. Almost everything I was coming into contact with was edible.

"Clover!" I heard Kylie yell.

"Clover?" Logan questioned.

I barked to let them know where I was. I hadn't gone far. I wasn't quite done with the trash, though.

They came around the corner and looked at me. I looked back at them and remembered being in this very spot when I first saw Logan.

"Clover, what are you doing?" Kylie asked as she started to approach me. "Are we not feeding you enough?"

"I'm pretty sure she just has a thing for scavenging," Logan said to Kylie.

"I guess so," Kylie replied to Logan. "As long as it's not happening in the house, I guess we're good."

Kylie turned back toward me.

"Let's go, girl, it's starting to rain," Kylie said with some eagerness in her voice.

I finished the last piece of food that I'd been working on and thought about how I'd come to accept my time as Rain, but now understood the term to simply be a word for wet weather. I looked back at Logan and Kylie as water started to fall on my fur. I had no urge to run away like I used to when someone spotted me at a trash container, before Logan and Kylie had come into my new life as Clover. As much as I loved pieces of my life before I left my first home, I knew this was where I was meant to be now.

"Come on, Clover," Kylie called again, a bit louder, but still in her sweet voice.

I was already on my way, leaving the alley behind as I trotted back to them.

"Let's go, girl," Kylie said as she opened the back door of her car. "Logan has to get to work."

Logan bent down to pet me, and I relished in his scent one last time before hopping in the back of Kylie's car.

"It was good to see you," I could hear Logan say to Kylie. "Thanks for stopping by."

"Of course," Kylie replied.

I watched as they smushed their faces together again. I wasn't as surprised by their display this time, so I stayed quiet in Kylie's car, letting the couple enjoy their idyllic moment. Kylie must've enjoyed it more this time because Logan smelled so good.

Afterwards, I watched Logan walk into the building behind him while Kylie joined me in her car. I stretched out in the back seat, content and relaxed. Even though Logan didn't join us, I now knew Kylie had just as hard of a time staying away from him as I did, so I wasn't worried about when I'd see him again.

So much had changed since Logan and I had first met. In Logan, I had a new friend. And in Kylie, I had a new home. I took a deep breath to take in the remaining chicken scent that still lingered and was happy to have Kylie turn her car on, look back toward me, and say, "Let's go home, Clover."